THE A...

Isabelle Eberhardt was born in ... daughter of Russian exiles. Her mother, Mme N... Moerder, had deserted her husband, a general in Tsar Alexander II's court, to flee with her children's tutor, Alexander Trophimowsky, an anarchist and friend of Bakunin. Brought up as a boy by Trophimowsky, Isabelle spoke six languages, including Arabic, by the age of sixteen. She had articles published pseudonymously in Paris magazines, and conceived a passion for Islam, the desert and the nomadic way of life. By the end of the century, after the sudden deaths of her parents, she was free to live in North Africa, as she had long dreamed of doing. In the guise of a young Arab student, she travelled to the Algerian Sahara, shocking the French settlers with her libertine way of life, but gaining the respect of the local sheikhs. Already a Muslim, she now became a member of a Sufi sect. In 1901 an assassination attempt on her led to a celebrated trial. In the same year she married a young Arab sergeant, and lived a life of poverty and persecution for two years, before being sent to the Algerian-Moroccan border to report for an Algerian newspaper on General Lyautey's campaign in Morocco. After a retreat in a Moroccan monastery she returned, ill, to the military base at Aïn Sefra. The day after discharging herself from hospital there, she was drowned in a flash flood on 21 October 1904. She was twenty-seven.

During Isabelle's lifetime scores of her articles and stories about North Africa were published. They were collected posthumously into books: *Dans l'ombre chaude de l'Islam* (1906), *Notes de route* (1908), *Pages d'Islam* (1920), *Contes et paysages* (1923), and *Au pays des sables* (1944). Her diaries (*Mes Journaliers*) were published in 1944 and her novel *Trimardeur (Vagabond)* in 1922. This is its first appearance in English.

VAGABOND

Isabelle Eberhardt

Translated by
Annette Kobak

THE HOGARTH PRESS
LONDON

Published in 1988 by
The Hogarth Press
30 Bedford Square
London WC1B 3RP

First published in French (as *Trimardeur*) by Fasquelle 1922
Translation and Introduction copyright © Annette Kobak 1988

A CIP catalogue record for this book is available from the
British Library

ISBN 0 7012 0823 6

Photoset in Linotron Sabon and Plantin by
Rowland Phototypesetting Ltd
Bury St Edmunds, Suffolk
Printed in Great Britain by
Cox and Wyman Ltd
Reading, Berkshire

INTRODUCTION

Although Isabelle Eberhardt's novel *Trimardeur* (*Vagabond*) was unfinished at her sudden death in the flash flood at Aïn Sefra in October 1904, most of it had appeared in instalments between August 1903 and July 1904 in the Algiers-based newspaper *L'Akhbar*, run by her friend and colleague Victor Barrucand. After July, Isabelle had shelved the novel, feeling that she needed time to work on the ending and to expand the chapters on Geneva, and had concentrated instead on the articles which she was writing for *L'Akhbar* under the general title 'Sud-Oranais'.

Her attitude reflected a change in her circumstances. The current of 'contemplative nihilism' which, as Barrucand said, had run through both her life and her novel, had been interrupted by her despatch in October 1903 to the embattled regions of the south-west Algerian frontier, where General Lyautey was masterminding a French advance into Morocco. To be thrust into the world of action was powerfully attractive to Isabelle, after an adolescence marked by parental ambivalence, immobilising idealism and plain gloom. Isabelle's brief was to follow the army, reporting – in objective, diplomatic terms – on the skirmishes and strategy for *L'Akhbar*. In doing so, she was discovering new resources within herself which would need time to assimilate into the novel. She also went into a spiritual retreat in a monastery in Kenadsa in Morocco for the summer of 1904, which brought new, rueful insights into her own nature and into what she felt was her destiny. And so Dmitri Orschanow, her hero in *Vagabond*, whose quest for a free life so closely mirrored Isabelle's own, was left suspended in the Foreign Legion – the refuge of romantic souls yearning for action and oblivion – while the drama of her own life took over. Had Isabelle lived longer than her short twenty-seven years, the influence of these two episodes, of war and of peace, would doubtless have affected the course of Dmitri's narrative, and his occasionally glib romanticism.

As it was, *Vagabond* remained unfinished and unrevised at her death. It is essentially a *Bildungsroman*, following the sentimental and worldly education of an idealistic, troubled young Russian medical student as he seeks a way of life which satisfies his need to live as a free individual, untrammelled by the conventions of society. The student Dmitri is based not only on Isabelle herself, but also on her older brother Augustin, who joined the Foreign Legion in 1895 and wrote Isabelle detailed accounts of his life there for a novel they planned to write together. As a result, the narrative does not always transcend the autobiographical, and occasionally gets caught up in turgid and unresolved moralising, as Isabelle leads Dmitri into episodes which confront him with the dilemmas she was wrestling with at various stages of her life: individual emancipation versus collective libertarian dogma (with its implied contradictions); love versus lust; study versus 'the great book of the universe'; western striving versus eastern fatalism and 'drifting on the tide of life' (Isabelle's draft title for the book was 'Adrift' [*A la dérive*]; before that it had been 'The Way' [*La voie*]).

But the public interest in Isabelle which followed her untimely death (some of it engineered by Barrucand himself as he sought to exoticise her image for Parisian readers) became such that Barrucand eventually published *Trimardeur* in 1922, adding an invented ending of his own. In it, he tried to bring the tale neatly back to its beginning, making Dmitri reflect that he left Vera and the 'warm little cage of happiness' because he needed the high road of life, with its diversity of passions. Barrucand then had Dmitri write a (banal) note to Vera saying that he is happy, that he did the right thing in leaving her, and that he wishes her well.

However, Isabelle had in fact drafted her own ending to the story, which can be found presented as a short story, 'Le Russe', in the posthumous collection *Pages d'Islam*. It is this ending, in slightly abridged form, rather than Barrucand's, which I have given the present translation. It, too, is abrupt, and not as satisfying as one can imagine Isabelle's writing might have been after her experiences on the Moroccan borders and in Kenadsa, but it is undoubtedly a more fitting end to Dmitri's picaresque wanderings than is Barrucand's flat coda.

Even so, *Vagabond* remains in many ways a flawed novel. The bravado Isabelle has Dmitri exhibit when he addresses a political meeting of dockers in Marseilles, or when he confronts a rough soldier in the Foreign Legion, is a reflection of her own wishful thinking (and an intimation of a shy side to her, running counter to the dash and braggadocio of her image). Dmitri's agonised broodings on the nature of freedom can seem trite, and his justification of the brutal side of his nature alarmingly naive and self-deluding; and certainly Isabelle cannot claim to have broken new philosophic ground with her meditations on liberty and happiness. In addition, Dmitri's musings are mostly un-mitigated by any authorial irony, and are often exacerbated by purple prose.

But even these failures are interesting, for if Isabelle occasionally lapses into the grandiose, it is as a result of having tackled a grand theme, that of an individual's liberty, whether man or woman. And even if no account is taken of the extraordinary life she was leading while writing the book, Isabelle's achievements in the novel are considerable.

Vagabond is notable firstly for its scope. Other contemporary women writers undoubtedly wrote better than Isabelle, but none had her unprecedented range of experience, most of which was almost exclusively the province of men (and some of which remains so). Thanks to the fact that she had been brought up, on vaguely anarchist principles, as a boy, and was used to appearing in public in male dress, she could write at first hand of being a medical student, an anarchist, a Marseilles docker, a vagabond, and from her own observation, as well as from her brother's notes, about the Foreign Legion. Moreover, like Mary Wollstonecraft, she inherited that unusual thing for the nineteenth century, an avant-garde background, and as a result her short life touched directly on matters of international moment: the first rumblings of what would become the Russian Revolution, the International Socialist movement, colonialism, the pan-Islamic movement. As a result, Isabelle's canvas is resolutely undomestic. Her fellow Russian Marie Bashkirtseff, with whom Isabelle has certain affinities, yearned to act and think in the emancipated, accountable way that Isabelle was to do. Bashkirtseff wrote: 'What I long for is the freedom of going about alone . . . and that's the freedom without which one cannot become a real artist.' Isabelle, thanks to her disguise, simply took the historically precocious freedom of going about alone, and *Vagabond* is in one sense a meditation on the price any individual (regardless of sex) has to pay for that freedom.

Isabelle's view, which she acted out to the full in her own life, is expressed in Dmitri's contention that 'it would be far better if everyone just took all possible moral, intellectual and material liberties right now, from today onwards, regardless of the sanctions of modern society. Let each individual emancipate him or herself. General emancipation won't come any other way.' The character of Anntone Ossipow (who was modelled on Isabelle's tutor and unacknowledged father, the anarchist Alexander Trophimowsky) puts her credo in more spiritual terms: 'Nothing matters, except the sincere and simple search for the right path.'

Because of its subject matter, *Vagabond* stands as a unique period piece. Isabelle vividly conveys the feel of young anarchist gatherings around the samovar, or the sights and smells of turn-of-the-century Marseilles, or the sweaty, gaslit, excited throng of dockers milling through the dark streets of the port protesting their right to work, or the futile, confused, punishing life of the Foreign Legion, with its occasional moments of redeeming camaraderie, or the seedy, gaudy, lively Arab parts of the military-dominated southern Saharan oases.

Yet, although Dmitri's narrative closely follows Isabelle's own exceptional life, the novel belongs essentially to the tradition of Russian literature. With its vagabond hero, close to nature, and in its plumbing of what Nabokov dismissively calls 'the depths of the good old Russian soul,' *Vagabond* is unmistakably Russian. Through Trophimowsky's teaching, Isabelle was familiar from childhood with the great Russian writers of the nineteenth century. While Dostoevsky, 'the poet of moral decay and human suffering,' was her favourite among them, the example of the life and work of one of Trophimowsky's own heroes, the 'gentle anarchist' Tolstoy, undoubtedly left its mark on Isabelle's thinking. Tolstoy's learning of Arabic (in 1844), his writing from the Crimean War, his idealisation of the Tatar, his adoption of Rousseau's plea for a return to nature, to honest work and simplicity, all have their echoes in Isabelle's life. Tolstoy's ideas in turn had grown out of the literary and political climate of the time in Russia, with writers like Turgenev (in *Sportsman's Tales*), Grigorovitch and Goremika all dealing sympathetically with the life of the Russian peasant, which was to become such a cult in Russia in the second half of the nineteenth century – particularly amongst those exiles who, like Isabelle, were themselves far removed from the *moujik*. (The *moujik*, the Tatar and the vagabond occupied much the same position within Russian literature of the time as the Red Indian does in twentieth-century American literature.)

In spite of the fact that Isabelle never lived in Russia, and wrote *Vagabond* in French, her novel grew from Russian soil, and its place (though, it must be conceded, not its literary stature) lies somewhere between Tolstoy's 1863 story 'The Cossacks', with its thesis that culture is the enemy of happiness ('The rougher [the peasants] were, the fewer were there any signs of civilisation, the freer he felt') and Gorky's *The Lower Depths*, first performed in 1902 ('You don't belong anywhere. Nobody on earth belongs anywhere.' 'A man must root himself in his place, not go traipsing aimlessly about the face of the earth.'). It is also worth noting that *Vagabond* predates by seven years Conrad's haunting and masterly *Under Western Eyes*, which is centred around the anarchist milieu in Geneva in which Isabelle grew up. Conrad's narrator's comment that: 'I saw then the shadow of autocracy lying upon Russian lives in their submission or their revolt' would be an appropriate epigram for *Vagabond*, and underlines its Russian roots.

However, *Vagabond* is also simply a good story. There is the occasional phrase ('the subdued light, pale as a convalescent's smile') or piece of characterisation (the stolid but appealing Perrin, eternally embarrassed by his Swissness) which makes one regret that Isabelle did not live to develop her writing talent, enriched as it would have been by the extraordinary, but chastening, adventures of her last year.

Annette Kobak, Cheltenham 1988

PART ONE

I

In the corner of the room a silver nightlight hung in front of an ancient triptych, a marvel of Byzantine art. The old gold of the shrine gleamed feebly in its glow, giving a strange halo to the emaciated faces of Christ, Mary and the apostles. In the middle of the room, two large lamps illuminated a table set with a red tablecloth, tea-glasses, and a copper samovar which was just coming to the end of its plaintive little chant. Some twenty people were talking loudly, with the almost violent excitement common to Russian discussions. Yet you could sense one spirit uniting these poorly-dressed young men, some in embroidered peasant blouses, and these young women in plain black dresses, leaning on their elbows amongst the men in a comradely way.

The head of the house, the neo-Christian philosopher Anntone Ossipow, smiled at these children of a different generation, with different ideas, who were meeting in the safety of his house. Strongly-built, and with a huge white beard which spread over his peasant's *poddiovka*, Ossipow stayed calm, barely joining in the conversation, although his large blue eyes would sometimes flicker with a soft inner light. A gentle anarchist of Tolstoyan bent, a disciple of his own particular Christ, he had distributed his considerable fortune among the local peasants. Then he had taken refuge in this old suburban house outside St Petersburg, where he now spent his days interpreting the Scriptures and making a living from the humble trade of bookbinding. He loved revolutionary youth, without sharing its convictions. What did differences of dogma matter, since these new spirits were, like him, engaged in a passionate search for truth, and dreaming of an ideal of justice?

Dmitri Orschanow, a medical student, kept quiet and a little aloof from the others. To him the discussions were becoming increasingly tedious, and the company of the other students tiresome. If someone addressed him directly, he could barely suppress a quick shrug of impatience. Yet once he had been among the most committed of the revolutionaries. Together with two or three others, he had founded an action committee to help prisoners escape from Siberian camps, and until quite recently he had been the very soul of the group. But now, although he hadn't actually changed his beliefs, he was losing all energy and all will to act. Instead he felt an agonising need for solitude, inactivity and silence. He knew that he might end up being suspected of betrayal, and the thought filled him with distaste: were these libertarians going to turn into tyrants, to hold on to him by force? Wasn't he free to go as he had come, to return into obscurity and silence?

Orschanow, who belonged to the robust race of Oriental Russians, was, at twenty-four, tall and strong. But recently his health had weakened, and his fine, spiritual Slav features had become drawn. Under the chestnut hair which fell over his forehead, his brown eyes had taken on a sad and anxious look.

A young woman now joined them. Tall and slender in her blue dress, she had a beautiful face which radiated quiet, kindly energy. The close-cut black curls falling across her high forehead cast a shadow across the lustre of her large grey eyes. Old Ossipow gave the young woman an affectionate hug. 'My children,' he said, 'meet Vera Gouriewa, my niece.' They already knew of her by reputation. Her father, an aristocrat who had a government

4

post in the south-east, had calculatingly married a rich tradeswoman, Agrafena Ossipow – old Anntone's sister – and had always regretted this expedient and demeaning marriage. He never loved his wife, and had kept her hidden in the house, never introducing her into society. When she had died young, leaving him Vera, Gouriewa had wanted to bring up his daughter according to the conventions of his class. But a governess, telling Vera of the appalling misery that existed among the people she came from, had kindled an independent spirit and a passionate fighter's soul in the girl.

At eighteen Vera had come to Petersburg against her father's wishes. Living with her uncle, she had started to study medicine, but then married a Bulgarian colleague, Stoïlow. Both were very young, and dreamt of sharing a common vocation. But soon Stoïlow, who was a feeble and indecisive character, fell in with the terrorist party. He was inspired by the idea of propaganda through action, but lacked the moral strength to carry out any courageous act himself. This powerlessness drove him to despair, and from then on Vera's own moral stability became a torment and a constant reproach to her husband, in spite of her affection for him. One day, Stoïlow begged his wife for a separation, on the pretext of the incompatibility of their natures, but really from remorse at making her suffer unnecessarily. It was agreed, and they had parted without rancour, as good friends.

After that, as a result of her involvement in student agitation at the university, Vera had been exiled to the Siberian frontier. She had asked to be sent as a nurse to Tioumène, where Russians were being sent on their way to the vast uncultivated lands of Siberia. Now after two years she had arrived back from this first contact with the common people, filled with compassion and energy, and was about to return to her interrupted studies.

Everyone in the room stood up. They introduced themselves and shook her hand in a welcome which was almost an ovation, since they all knew of her selflessness and heroism in the hell of Siberia. Stoïlow was there too, and also greeted her warmly. They pressed her to tell them about her experiences, which she did simply and self-effacingly, telling of the crowds of people herded together in smoky, airless *izbas*, men, women, children and invalids all thrown together in such congestion and filth that epidemics were rife. She spoke of the criminal negligence and the treacherousness of the administration, and of its perverse and fierce hostility towards the few intellectuals who, like her, were trying to do some good and create a little order. No hospital, no medications, the few doctors reduced to helplessness through overwork, the cemetery bursting and overflowing into the nearby fields, scattering its harvest of little black crosses ... A deep silence fell, and sadness hung in the bright room like a sigh of distress. But Vera shook her black curls in a determinedly nonchalant gesture. 'Well, we mustn't allow ourselves to despair. People are really *living* there, in that constant struggle between fear and willpower! Fighting is good: it's a healthy and energising atmosphere.'

Orschanow had been staring at her ever since she came in, and now admiration and something like envy welled up in him in the face of this beautiful creature. He found himself attracted to Vera simply because she was healthy, a life-force, and because he felt himself to be so pitifully weak, so indecisive, so full of bitter self-disgust. He looked at Stoïlow in astonishment: he was so thin, so yellow, with such a bilious and fevered look. How had the love and

6

constant companionship of a woman like this not redeemed him? And as he thought of his own solitude, and of the abandonment in which he had grown up, and still lived, self-pity welled up in him.

Dmitri's father, Nikita Orschanow, had been a member of the government in Samara. He was a utopian, full of humanitarian ideas, who had ruined himself with expensive new horticultural schemes which used all the latest equipment to no avail, and were doomed to failure. He had married a poor teacher of Tatar origin, Lisa Mamontow, who had died giving birth to Dmitri. Dmitri's older brother Vassily, a sensible little fellow even when he was ten years old, had managed to get himself sent off to live with an aunt in Moscow, leaving Dmitri alone in the care of the servants.

Very early on he had become a dreamer, loving to lose himself for hours on end in the silence of the vast house and in the overgrown garden, where hazel trees, mountain ash and gloomy hollies formed a thick undergrowth beneath the forest oaks, limes and delicate, white-trimmed birches. A pond lay in the shadows, still and overgrown with weeds, with all the troubling mystery of stagnant waters. The trees sloped down gradually, masking the view, then stopped abruptly, and there was the wide, slow Volga flowing in the sunlight. On the left bank, beyond the little village of Petchal, were the endless steppes, the free steppes, with their grasses billowing from one horizon to the next, and in the distant haze you could make out high, tree-covered cliffs.

Nikita Orschanow spent months in his far-off estates, leaving Dmitri alone. As soon as the boy got out of school, he would disappear into the garden or the steppes. It was there he had spent the best years of his childhood, lost in wordless reverie, in the soft melancholy and sombre silence of this vast northern landscape. Occasionally an eagle would soar above the steppes, and then hover in mid-air, and Dmitri loved to watch the continuous shimmering of the bird's wild wings in the sunlight. Then an almost painful longing would come over him — a desire to intoxicate himself with space, to run through the steppes, on and on, towards the dreamlands he sensed beyond the blue wall of the horizon. Later, he discovered river life, befriending the sailors and *bourlaki*, the tugboatmen of the river port. He loved the noisy towpaths, the smell of resin in amongst the sturdy northern trees, trees which would be cut down and made into barges to travel down the life-giving Volga to the southern towns in spring. Dmitri used to spell out these distant, evocative names to himself, Saratow, Tsaritsyn, Astrakan . . . The first time he watched the *bourlaki* setting off, to the accompaniment of the prayers and solemn chanting of the clergy, he almost wept, overcome by a new emotion. They sang, too, these *bourlaki*, on their flag-decked barges. Oh, those songs of freedom, of infinite sadness, of daring! They awakened a whole world of yearning in Dmitri's solitary heart, bewitching him and giving him forever afterwards a thirst for the travelling life. Oh, to set off, to set off to the most distant of distant lands, not as a *tourist*, not as a rich and idle man of leisure, but as a poor and rough sailor. Oh, to set sail, to leave! Dmitri didn't envy Pierre Ivanovitch Rostow, the local lord of the manor, who, they said, had visited the whole of Europe. The people whose lives attracted him were the *stranniki*, the vagabonds, pilgrims and vagrants, and the gypsies, and sailors, and *bourlaki*.

Ever since he had started school, Dmitri had hated its regimentation and cloistered tedium, and had often come close to expulsion for his rebellious attitude. He studied unenthusiastically, merely to please his father, whom he loved with a strange, almost subliminally sad love. Even as a small child he had felt an anguished pity and sympathy for anything which suffered, and above all for the poor, for the peasants, for animals. Later on, in school, his indignation at any injustice had drawn him to friends with libertarian ideas. It was at about this time that he had discovered an old library in a disused wing of his father's house piled high with long-forgotten, dusty books and manuscripts. He had been particularly taken by some books on ethnography left there by his uncle, Dr Vladimir Orschanow, who had been exiled to Siberia for his liberal opinions and had eventually died there, leaving his books and research to his brother Nikita. Dmitri spent every evening reading and studying in the library, revelling in the old-fashioned décor and hangings, faded and mellowed by twenty years of abandon. He developed a passionate interest, almost a cult, for this martyred uncle he had never known, and decided to follow in his footsteps, to become a doctor like him, and to work for a cause. In all sincerity he believed that he had discovered the same humanitarian vocation in himself, and enrolled in the faculty of medicine in St Petersburg, full of hope and energy. Learning came easily to him, and for the first two years he worked hard and conscientiously. From the start he took part in all the revolutionary meetings and projects, but he soon found that the socialist ideal didn't suit his nature. His ideas were changing and developing, and finally he gave his full allegiance to the anarchists, with their demand of complete freedom for the individual.

For a while, in spite of his youth, he became a ringleader, starting up several action committees, including the

Siberian committee, which planned and abetted several celebrated escapes. He had been happy in this period of his student life. His need for an integrated life was satisfied, he was *living*, with all his nervous energy, with all his will-power, without understanding the danger of the frenetic life he was leading. But then, saturated with activity, he imperceptibly began to tire of it, and his overwrought nerves began to relax, after too much tension. He sensed that his life was becoming less intense, less vibrant, and, thinking that he'd been overdoing things and getting exhausted, he decided that if he took a break, everything would get better. During the summer holidays he took refuge in a small village outside the city, and it was there that his path changed definitively. The sunny plain, the woods and the sad horizon captivated him again. He rediscovered all the pleasurable longings of his childhood, the yearnings for some unknown elsewhere . . . Then, alarmed, he had returned to St Petersburg, and tried to force himself to work. But the student life, his revolutionary activity, the meetings, had lost their charm. Morose boredom took over from his previous frenzied enthusiasm.

When he had first arrived in St Petersburg, Orschanow had wanted to study the urban slums, had even wanted to try to sow seeds there of newer, healthier ideas. He had become involved in the squalid life he discovered there as a preacher, an apostle of enlightenment. But when he came back from the country he found something else was drawing him back to the areas of misery, alcohol and prostitution: a dark need for suffering. Now he went there aimlessly, without any notion of research or proselytising: the sordidness attracted him, and he felt an agonising need to give in to it completely. He identified with the derelicts he rubbed shoulders with, human wrecks who dragged out their lives there, as low as could be, despised, ragged and kicked underfoot.

Sometimes he did try to resist, in a final spasm of everything which had been his reason for living for the past eight years. He didn't want to admit that the vocation he had fondly imagined didn't exist, or that his character as a man of science and action was totally fabricated.

It was in this vague and troubled state of mind that he had come here to this meeting, or rather that he had forced himself to come, in spite of himself. But, after hearing Vera talk, he felt ashamed of his weakness and of what he still thought of as his cowardice. This beautiful, calm fighter, who knew her own strength and enjoyed it, rekindled Dmitri's energy and his need for action.

*

Towards one o'clock the groups broke up in the road outside. The summer night, white as an uncertain dawn, was mild and lightly scented with lilac, and the air was good and sweet in the silence of the empty avenues. Abruptly Orschanow left his companions, going off on his own, slowly, feeling a sort of appeased tenderness, a sudden relief, as if a crushing weight had been lifted from him. What! At twenty-four years old, with all the energy he had so often felt coursing through his whole being, with his intelligence, which he knew was acute, how had he arrived at this shameful inertia, at this pathetic snivelling about his life? No, he had to shake himself out of it, and overcome his nerves, which were as enfeebled as some invalid woman's, and once more be the person whose determination and daring used, until quite recently, to astonish his friends. And wasn't Vera his predestined soulmate, whose courage and moral health he could draw on from now on?

Orschanow returned almost joyfully to his bare room, full of dust and disorder, in the eaves of the large, gloomy, ivy-covered house.

2

The members of the Siberian committee were meeting at Arseny Makarow's house, an old photographic studio. Books and surgical instruments were scattered pell-mell on the tables and chairs, and the evening warmth wafted through the windows. Makarow, a giant of a man with blue eyes and a thick blonde fleece of hair, strode up and down the room nervously, his hands stuffed into his blue peasant's belt.

The group was composed of Vera Gouriewa, who had just joined the committee, Marie Garchina, a small, crippled primary school teacher, Emilie Himmelschein, a beautiful redheaded Jewess with a serene, serious face, Hospodian, a dark Armenian with darting, coal-fire eyes and self-consciously tragic airs, Davidow, a consumptive, with a morose and troubled look, and little Rioumine, who had barely left school and was still almost beardless, but had a hard, unsmiling face and striking iron-grey eyes flaming with intelligence and will-power.

'What the devil do you mean? It's absurd!' Makarow cried excitedly. 'Orschanow a traitor! It's idiotic. Tell me, Gouriewa, and you, Rioumine – you two are the calmest of us all – and you Himmelschein, you know Orschanow well – does he give you the impression of being a traitor?'

Vera was smoking silently. She smiled. 'I've only seen Orschanow once or twice. And then he hardly opened his mouth. All I can say is that nothing in his face or manner seems suspicious to me.'

'Nor in his actions either,' Emilie Himmelschein interjected with feeling.

Davidow, who had organised this meeting, protested. 'But God help me, I never said Orschanow was a traitor! It's just that I said and I say again that he is completely distancing himself from us.'

'Yes, it's true,' Garchina cried in her shrill invalid's voice, 'and he knows all the committee's secrets and many more besides! Davidow is right, it's beginning to get dangerous.'

Hospodian tilted his chair backwards and declared sententiously: 'Either with us, or against us.'

Emilie Himmelschein flung her cigarette down angrily. 'Heaven knows what you're all saying! Can't you see Orschanow is in some distress, that he's being troubled by something we don't know about? You must have caught the old guard's mania for plots, to be getting suspicious of a comrade for a simple change of behaviour!'

Makarow broke in excitedly: 'Don't you understand that, on the contrary, if he wanted to betray us he wouldn't be distancing himself from us so obviously, with no explanation?' Makarow wasn't a friend of Orschanow's, and had no relationship with him outside the committee. But it was in his nature to get worked up like this whenever a cause seemed right to him. He roundly challenged those who seemed to be incriminating Dmitri: 'All right then, what should we do, according to you? Should we do away with him, like they do in all the good nihilist stories?'

13

Davidow went pale. 'Oh, Makarow, you're being unfair! Who said anything about that? It's simply that this matter has got to be brought out into the open.'

'If one of us were *convicted* of treason, yes, we would have to get rid of him, because there would be no other way of stopping him from destroying everything – all of us, our work, and the poor wretches who believe in us out there in Siberia, and whose lives are in our hands. But we should need to be absolutely certain before we pronounced such a sentence! In the present case, there isn't even a serious probability at the moment. We must look into the matter, and then decide.' Rioumine had spoken drily and unemotionally, with his usual concern for strict fairness, but Davidow's manner was still so involuntarily aggressive that Vera smiled again.

'Take my advice, Davidow, and let me speak with him. In his present state of mind you won't get anything out of him. You mustn't get so heated.'

Orschanow returned from an aimless walk through the streets to find an unsigned scrap of paper slipped under his door: 'Ten o'clock, at my place, urgent.' A mark in the corner told him it was from Makarow. Dmitri was startled, and then felt sudden anger. This was the interrogation, the calling to heel, which he had been expecting for some time. Betrayal brought in its wake unavoidable penalties. It was a question of life or death.

He flung himself on his bed fully dressed. He thought of the committee members ... Davidow, Garchina and Hospodian would be inclined to accuse him. The others ... How could he know? Weren't they devoted, almost fanatical, and wasn't the danger that was being presented to them serious, and their responsibility heavy? If they felt absolutely *sure* of his guilt, he would be killed. He sensed

14

that he wouldn't have anything to say to them that could explain or defend his conduct, but would end up being aggressive and violent, and alienating them. Lacking the courage to go to Vera, he fell into pointless self-torment. On top of all this, he had been going without food recently and was getting anaemic. He had barely any money left, and his father could no longer help him out, since he was now quite bankrupt. Dmitri didn't even try to earn some money, as the others did, by giving lessons or doing translations. He went to bed in the dark, without eating, waiting for ten o'clock to come. He began to think wistfully of Vera. The thought that she was one of those who would pass judgement on him held a curious appeal. His anger and rebelliousness faded as he thought that if he were condemned, she would have had a hand in his death.

*

At ten o'clock Orschanow went to Makarow's. As soon as he arrived he was aware of the awkwardness and anxiety around him. The committee members shook his hand in silence, their faces pale and worried. Orschanow remained standing. Once again anger and bitterness welled up inside him. He said fiercely, 'You called for me! Here I am. What do you want from me?'

Vera spoke quietly. 'Sit down, Orschanow. You are well aware of the seriousness of the mutual interests that bind us together. I don't need to remind you of the responsibility we all bear. Well, we've all noticed such a change in your attitude that we've called you here for an explanation.'

'Out with it! Just say you suspect me of treachery!'

Orschanow's voice shook with distress, and his expression darkened. His words left an icy silence behind them.

But Makarow leapt to his feet. 'No one suspects you! You've been the bravest and most active of us. Who would dare insult you like that?'

Davidow could no longer contain himself. 'Yes, it's true you've been the most admirable of all of us. But now you're leading a mysterious life. You hardly ever come to meetings, you don't involve yourself in anything, and then you disappear for weeks on end. Whenever we come to you on urgent business, you're never there, or you pretend not to be there. You must admit it all seems pretty strange.'

Orschanow suddenly felt his pride piqued, as he used to at school. 'What right have you got to dictate to me? You call yourselves anarchists and yet you want to set up the worst kind of tyranny by judging and spying on a man's private life! I take exception to this presumption, do you understand?'

Emilie Himmelschein came up to him. 'Orschanow, my dear, don't get angry. You know that Davidow cannot speak calmly. We're simply asking why you've abandoned the group's interests.'

Dmitri might have calmed down at that point, but then Garchina butted in: 'We haven't got a private life, we belong entirely to the common cause. You have to justify your behaviour.'

Dmitri got up. 'Well, no, I'm not going to. I've got nothing to say. If you think I'm a traitor then get rid of me. Because that's what you've got to decide, isn't it? If you're worried about it then spy on me, find out for yourselves what I am, if you're clever enough. But I object to being judged by you and I'm leaving for good.'

Rioumine quietly blocked his exit. Vera had got up, and

she forced Orschanow to sit down again, leaving her hand on his shoulder. He looked up at her; she seemed very far away, and a kind of bliss came over him. Makarow saw tears in Dmitri's eyes and was moved, turning against the others suddenly. 'You're inhuman! Our comrade is suffering in some way – how do you know he's not in real trouble? And you're tormenting him more, in the sacred name of your prejudices!'

Vera was upset, since she could see from Orschanow's face that he was very far from having the ideas they were ascribing to him. She turned and challenged them all: 'Will those who suspect Orschanow speak out plainly now!' There was a silence. 'There. You can see no one has anything to say. I'll explain your attitude to them myself. Your thoughts are elsewhere, you've got some private worry, some personal preoccupation which is distancing you from our affairs. That's all. You need some rest. So we shan't make it worse for you. Let's have done with this painful scene. We – Himmelschein, Makarow and I – shall be your guarantors. If you want to leave the committee for a while, do so. You have every right to reclaim your freedom.'

Orschanow got up. 'I thank those of you who have had the courage to act as free men . . . Now let me go for the time being. If ever I am able to come back, I shall do so. If not, adieu!' He left the room awkwardly, without shaking hands with anyone.

Faced with Vera's self-confidence and calm, the other members of the committee had backed down out of respect for her well-known integrity. There was silence for a while, and then Makarow spoke his thoughts out loud: 'He's right, we must act like free men. What's the point of all these Dumas *père* scenes, all these committees with a president, a vice-president and so on, all this puerile and illogical imitation of just those forms of government which we're attacking?'

*

Oschanow went back to his room in a fevered state, prey to feelings of bitter irritation and revolt. How dare they try to control his private life, to delve into his painful inner secrets? It exasperated him. The suspicious faces of Davidow, Garchina and the Armenian seemed to leer at him through his lucid delirium.

Yet four of them had had the courage to alleviate his suffering . . . Vera above all, and her image managed to calm him down. He wasn't alone any longer, because there was Vera. Sooner or later, when he could, he would go and see her.

3

After a night of fitful sleep Orschanow spent most of the next day in a state of indecision. Should he go to Vera's? Shame held him back. How could he tell her that for six months he had been living in the most sordid of lodgings, getting drunk with prostitutes and convicts, consciously wallowing in the mire – and that he *enjoyed* it?

What decided him to stay was the clear sense he had that, even if he confessed everything to Vera and she understood, at five o'clock he would nevertheless return in spite of everything to Goutouyew Island, to the poorest of the port areas, and find his mistress Polia. And when he was with her, inevitably, they would go to the public house and get drunk. So since he would still be a squalid creature, a wretched dog, who found the gutter's black mud delectable, what point was there in going and play-acting, as he called it bitterly, with Vera?

*

Polia was perhaps twenty years old. Her blonde hair surrounded a thin, suffering little face in which her large grey eyes, real Russian eyes, opened in astonishment and apprehension at the surrounding ugliness and misery. At sixteen she had started work at the paper factory owned by the Kozlow brothers. Her father and her stepmother drank and paid no attention to the girl. Polia had to suffer the promiscuities of the house and the working men. Before she was grown up she had, like all the other young girls around, been violated by the local men, and her health had been permanently damaged by a brutal succession of unheeding males. She had become passive, as if drugged, her dormant senses submitting to the men with resignation, as just another form of misery. In church, the priest kept repeating that fallen girls would burn forever in hell, but he never suggested a way of avoiding the debauchery which thrived on all sides.

Polia drank, like all the others, and she had got into the habit of prostituting herself for money after the exhaustion of the day. Occasionally she shook off her indifference, cursing her dog's life, and talked of doing what her sister Liouba had done, and working in old Ma Schmidt's brothel. At least there was enough to eat there, there was silk to dress in and warmth in winter, whereas at home there was only constant need since her brother Kolia had left for the army. One evening, as Orschanow was walking around the island, Polia had called out to him. Prey to one of his periodic fits of sensuality, and also lonely, he had followed her to a derelict warehouse.

Polia's senses had not yet been awakened. Dmitri's passionate love-making surprised her and made her smile. As for Dmitri, he became fond of her, because she epitomised for him the suffering and misery in which he liked to lose himself.

Polia was known on the island as 'Tatters' because her clothes were always so torn and dirty; she spent everything she earned from work and whoring on brandy. Gradually, as he began to succumb to the seductive, dark oblivion of drink, Orschanow had started to get drunk with Polia. She seemed to listen to him with distant, troubled eyes as he spoke drunkenly of things which were quite unintelligible to her. 'In her heart she understands me,' he assured himself, whenever Polia began to sob at seeing his tears.

The morning after his appearance before the Siberian committee, Orschanow decided against going to Vera's. Towards evening he went back to the desolate squalor of Goutouyew Island, through the labyrinth of dilapidated factories and sheds with broken windows as lugubrious as empty eye-sockets.

4

At first, people in this run-down area had been wary of Orschanow, sensing the young gentleman under his assumed rags. But gradually, with the innate sociability and desire for equality of the Russian people, undimmed by centuries of oppression, they accepted the ex-student. From the moment he got drunk out of 'pure despair', he had become one of them, and had the freedom of the city of the damned. To him it was a joy and an immense relief.

One day, having failed to find Polia, he had wandered aimlessly through the town, and found himself in Siennaya Square without realising it, in the cornmarket—Petersburg's Courtyard of Miracles, a rendezvous and refuge for prostitutes, criminals and the city's dregs.

Some drops of rain led Orschanow to shelter in an inn, a long room with smoky and shiny walls, like polished bronze. The owner was lording it in front of his rough wooden counter. He was a tall, robust young man with a dry, tanned face and black, slanting eyes: a Tatar. His forehead was shaved under his sheepskin bonnet, and his lithe body was clad in an old blue caftan, belted at the waist with a red sash. He claimed he was from Kazan and called himself Akhmatow, although his real name was Ahmetka, and he was a Muslim. A mood of high spirits and gaiety reigned in the place. Men played balalaikas and harmonicas, and girls in peasant scarves clattered in in their worn clogs to drink at the bar.

Orschanow sat down in a corner, observing the clientele with curiosity. At first sight these people could have passed for workmen, but Orschanow's experienced eye was not duped, and he congratulated himself quietly on having entered this bar. The observations and the friendships he could make here would break the monotony of his life and his wanderings in the slum areas.

From one of the groups near Orschanow, someone shouted out: 'Let's start a *maïdane*!' In the country Orschanow had often seen the *brodiaga*, escapees from Siberia who had become vagabonds. And this telltale word *maïdane*, which in Siberia means a card-game, told him at once what kind of place Akhmatow was running: a refuge for the *brodiaga*. He knew that most of the Siberian escapees were born vagabonds, men who were happy only on the highways, men for whom the only desirable life was the wandering life. He was at ease amongst them, and felt a need to get to know them and to speak with them.

Among those playing cards, Orschanow noticed a man of his own age, wearing a ragged caftan and an old fox-fur hat. He was a striking figure, in spite of his rags, tall and slim, with a regular, aquiline profile, wild eyes, dark brown hair, and an attractive, savage grace. His friends called him 'Oriol' (the Eagle). He was drinking a lot and, towards the end of the evening, an argument broke out between him and the owner over payment.

'Blockhead! Baldy!' shouted the Eagle.

'Yes, perhaps. And you? You reek of hard labour!'

'You'd know about that!'

'God alone knows if I'll come to that. But as for you, you're quite definitely there already!' Suddenly, with a sideways glance at Orschanow, they fell silent, and the Eagle paid up without any more fuss.

The next day, Orschanow returned to Akhmatow's with Petrow, an old workman from Goutouyew, a drunkard who had become what they ironically called in the slums a *valet de cœur*, a layabout. Petrow had developed a fondness for Dmitri and, since he was well known in Siennaya, Orschanow, as his companion, did not arouse suspicion any more. He was, it was true, a *barine*, an ex-student – but he had started to drink out of 'pure despair', and he preferred the company of the peasants to that of his well-educated or noble fellows. All they asked of him was that he shouldn't be a policeman, and Petrow's recommendation was enough to dispel any such suspicion. Contrary to the way things happen in the West, the ordinary Russian people have pity and sympathy for the *déclassés* who come among them.

The Eagle showed a crushing contempt for nearly all of Akhmatow's clientele, and for Akhmatow himself, whom he referred to as a pagan. But this particular evening, the Eagle came up to Orschanow and spoke to him, quizzing him about his past in short, dry sentences. The *brodiaga*'s wild eyes fixed on Dmitri's, saying clearly: 'Are you lying, or aren't you?' He evidently disdained to interrogate Petrow about the newcomer.

Orschanow always told the truth about himself and his life. Yet now he said he had definitely pledged himself to the 'Golden Legion' (as the poor and down-and-outs were ironically called). In fact, the idea did appeal to him, and he had been brooding over it in the melancholy of his solitary reveries.

The Eagle went so far in his courtesy as to offer Orschanow some brandy. Then they played cards, and, as Dmitri was losing, the Eagle threw his hand nonchalantly onto the table. 'You've had enough. If you still have a few kopecks, keep them for yourself.'

As they left, Petrow congratulated Orschanow. 'You managed to impress the Eagle. Well done! Very few people can claim to have drunk and played with him.' And the old workman told Dmitri what he could of the man he knew as Orlow.

He came originally from the Cossack land of the Urals, and as a very young man he had committed some crime of passion. He had been sent to Siberia, had escaped and become a *brodiaga*. They had caught him again, after a

23

new crime, this time an act of robbery. Every spring Orlow escaped, spurred on by his nostalgia for liberty in the woods and steppes. The year before he had fled Nerthschinsk, together with an old *brodiaga*. Just before Tioumène, the fugitives had hidden in an inn in the village of Neoplatimowka. One night they had overheard the owner and his son talking: the peasant was sending the young man to fetch the police to come and arrest the *brodiaga*. Orlow and his companion had cut the throats of the old man and his son, setting fire to the village before they left.

Yet this same Orlow had rescued a drowning woman from the river, and had always spared peasants who had given him hospitality and kept his secret. There was an odd mixture of pride, melancholy, cruelty and tenderness in him. One moment he would be getting drunk and violent and creating havoc, the next he would stay for weeks on end in some inn, plunged in a sort of mournful apathy. These details increased the curiosity and sympathy which Orschanow had felt for the Eagle since their first meeting.

When Orschanow confessed to the *brodiaga* that he knew a little about his background, the latter started violently. 'Watch it, by God! Oriol doesn't fool around.' But Orschanow shrugged his shoulders. Orlow spoke to him about Neoplatimowka, about the steppes and the forests. 'Listen,' said the *brodiaga*: 'Everyone here is a lackey, a flunkey always ready to lick the boots of anyone strong, or anyone who knows how to get respect. Most of them are miserable petty thieves. I've stolen too ... but not from people's pockets. As for them, they are cowards, in spite of the fact that their faces are not in the image of God. You see that I won't speak with them. Whereas I spoke to you because I saw you were unhappy. You don't belly-laugh like a beast when there's nothing funny and when men want to speak. But Miska, if you notice that I respect you, don't start thinking it's because of your knowledge. It's a man's heart which is important, not what he knows. All of us here are ignorant people, but those who have a heart don't need knowledge. Don't forget that.'

'When you fled, did you really go to the steppes?'

Orlow's eyes shone, and he smiled. 'Most of all the last time. It was right at the beginning of spring. I was with a butcher from Penu, who they called 'Golden-Knife'. The older people had recommended that we shouldn't go down to the south, to the area of the Chinese. They used to track down *brodiagas* to give them up to the Russian police. We'd left Nertschinsk and stayed hidden in a swamp for eight days, bitten by mosquitoes and shivering with fever. Every night the sound of the wind in the reeds made us tremble: we were terrified of being caught. Then we reached the forest. Ah, that was something else again. We slept on heather, underneath great oaks, and we ate fish which we caught with bent thorns and lines made from plaited grass, and game which we caught with home-made traps.'

The *brodiaga*'s wild eyes glistened at the memory, and he sat up. 'We went where we wanted to, freely, on God's land. We slept on dry leaves, on fine, sweet-smelling grass. When it was hot in the pine woods, there was the smell of incense, like in church.' He made a sweeping gesture. 'Everything was ours then, everything was our brother: the forest, the steppes, the streams, the great rivers ... Sometimes, we used to climb some huge tree and look at the forest from up there, all around us, right up to the point where the sky joins the earth. The wind used to roar at night, howling like wolves in the winter, and sometimes we used to press up against each other, God knows why.'

The *brodiaga*'s nostrils flared, and his powerful chest puffed out at these memories. 'If it had been up to me, I'd have stayed there. But the older men, like Golden-Knife, knew better and treated me like an idiot, asking me what I'd do in winter. So then we took the road to Russia. Near Tioumène, we got tangled up with the devil, taking yet more sin on our heads.'

'Yes, I know, you burnt down Neoplatimowka . . .'

The Eagle shot a long, piercing glance at Orschanow. 'Who told you that? And yet, I can see perfectly well that you won't go to the authorities and tell them . . . No, you wouldn't go.'

'How do you know I wouldn't go?'

'I'm like the fox or the three-legged beast,* I can sense hunting-dogs a mile off.'

'So, you burnt down Neoplatimowka?'

'Yes . . . You see, when we'd killed the old man and his son in order to save ourselves, I wanted to leave at once. But Golden-Knife said to me: "No, we've got to burn this damned village. This village here hasn't got God's stamp on it. We must burn those who rat on miserable wretches like us." '

'But where do you come from then, and is Orlow your real name?'

'Where do I come from? I'm no longer down there. My name? People call me Orlow, Oriol, Sachka-Bright-Eyes . . . Lots of names!'

The *brodiaga*'s face had suddenly darkened, and Orschanow did not press the point.

Since that evening, the Eagle had become Orschanow's

---

* A wolf, called three-legged because of its habit of running with one of its hind-legs lifted.

friend and companion. It was he who had initiated him into the secrets of Siennaya. It was a different world. The Eagle was at home in it. He knew everyone, he was respected and even admired. Everyone knew he was a *brodiaga* who had escaped from Siberia, and that increased his prestige.

Orschanow loved Siennaya. There you saw all sorts of people, wearing all types of clothes, and plying all kinds of trades. They sold anything. From dawn onwards the market-place was swamped with sellers setting up their wares, on benches, on planks, on the ground. Stallholders with mittens sold moth-eaten clothes, stale provisions, old eggs, roast liver, salted, smoked, dried or shrivelled fish. They cut up garlic, raw onion and black bread to cook on iron stoves, and workmen and scavengers came to get a bite to eat there for a few kopecks. Women threaded their way through the crowd with wooden boards on their heads laden with bread, shouting shrilly '*Zalatehi! Zalatchi!*' Nearby, people on their own, flotsam and jetsam, lay in halls or on benches instead of beds. In one corner was a rough, grease-covered table, some stacked canteen cutlery and painted wooden boxes containing workmen's clothes. In another corner was the enormous Russian brick pot which serves simultaneously for cooking and heating. In casement windows broken panes had been plugged with paper, or thin sheets of zinc, or rags. Workmen gathered there in the stink and clutter, without air or light.

Outside, countless puny, precocious children swarmed in plain cloth shirts. Women who before puberty had had a pale, delicate beauty, quickly grew old and ugly, with slack skins and drawn features. Prostitution and alcohol accounted for everything. This was the abominable Russian working-class, with derisory pay and the worst material and moral conditions. They represented the rot and decay of a whole people.

Orschanow no longer went there as a preacher. All he took down there, as he did to Siennaya when the Eagle was there, was his black despondency, drowning it in the vast and endless despair of these crushed, ugly people. He felt better among these people, less alone. No one reproached him for doing nothing, or for interminably propping up the bar where he liked to drink like everyone else. He sometimes found he had spent whole weeks in this way without going back to his room, spending the night anywhere, in whatever hovel he fell asleep in, dazed by alcohol and sloth, dead to the world.

5

It was nearly a month since Orschanow had appeared before the committee, and he still had not plucked up the courage to go to Vera's. Almost every day he thought of going, imagining the relief it would be if he could bare his heart to her and confess everything, if she would hold out a hand to him, become his friend. But then a sudden feeling of self-disgust would check him. Why go there, since he felt at home in the mire?

Yet, in moments of lucidity, Orschanow knew he wasn't happy, and that he couldn't go on like this. He drank, but he had not become a drunkard. He lived among layabouts and ex-convicts, but he did not feel he was becoming like them. What he needed in the grey mist of his present existence, what he longed for with his whole soul, with all the aching tension of his overstretched nerves, was a definitive solution. Somehow he had to resolve his future, either by becoming a student again, or by getting swallowed up forever as a workman or vagabond. What he must not do was to stay here in limbo, among these people defeated by life. He still loved life, he still needed light, pure air and space. He sensed it obscurely beneath his growing despair, and it was this which was pushing him irresistibly towards Vera.

*

Orschanow woke at dawn in the deserted building site where he had fallen asleep. The sun was rising full and red, and a pinkish glow passed over everything, like a veil of modesty. The air was warm and soft. In the silence of the still-deserted road, wild birds were waking, and a calm gaiety rose from this lost corner of the suburbs.

He had always been intensely affected by external things. Grey and rainy days threw him into gloom, while the least ray of sunshine revived him. That day, in the opal light of the morning, he was filled with a groundless joy, an almost agonised tenderness. Why was he letting himself give way to despair? Why was he rooting out a tormenting ugliness in people and things, when on the contrary he should be drinking in beauty and deeply inhaling the warm, invigorating air of daylight? So, at this early hour, he went to find Vera.

Her student's room, large and pale blue, and curtained with cheap white Indian fabric dotted with small pink flowers, contained only a narrow bed, a pine table, a desk, lockers and shelves loaded with books. Two open windows enjoyed a view on to a garden full of trees, whose branches dappled the sunlight flooding into the room.

Dressed in her simple, dark blue dress, Vera was just finishing correcting an article on the emigration of peasants from Siberia for a journal. As usual, she was smoking as she wrote rapidly in red ink. She showed no surprise when Orschanow came in.

'Welcome, Orschanow! But on one condition; you must sit down and stay still for five minutes. I'm very behind.'

Orschanow watched her working. Concentration lent her face something childlike and serious. She was hurrying, sometimes impatiently scoring out sections of the text, and as she bent over her manuscript her black curls fell over her forehead, giving her the delicate beauty of a young boy.

When she had finished, she smiled at Dmitri. 'I knew you would come one day. But where have you been since that last evening with us? Makarow and Himmelschein have been round to see you several times. They've always found the door open and the room empty. You don't look at all well. What's happened to you? You're someone who ought not to have too much solitude and silence. They're very dangerous for you! Come on, tell me what you've been doing since then?'

She guessed what was to come, anticipating a confession. It was a great relief to Orschanow, since he felt overcome with shame again, and he was thinking how ridiculous it was to come and tell his life story to this woman he scarcely knew.

Now, with a shy person's unintentional bluntness, he told her everything, from his old dreams on the banks of the Volga to his troubled wanderings of the past few months, even down to his liaison with Polia and his drunkenness. He left nothing out, making no attempt to gloss over the dark truth, or even to excuse himself.

'I understand it all. Except for one thing,' Vera said

thoughtfully. 'What was it that put you off student life so suddenly? What made you reject our moral credo, which used to be yours too? If you can explain that to me then perhaps I can tell you what I think you should do.'

'It was the monotony of that life which started to repel me. And then, subconsciously, I began to rebel against the duty my surroundings seemed to impose on me of being a man of social action. I love freedom, Gouriewa, and I didn't find freedom among our libertarians.'

'Well, of course not. We're not free. We're only humble workers for future freedom.'

'I used to think that too, once upon a time. But now it seems to me that it would be far better if everyone just took all possible moral, intellectual and material liberties now, from today onwards, regardless of the sanctions of modern society. Let each individual emancipate him or herself! General emancipation won't come any other way. Mind you, this is the first time I've tried to put this muddle of feelings and thoughts into words. It's also the first time I've talked about them to anyone.'

Vera remained thoughtful. 'But what do you call individual emancipation? Is it following your own lights without reference to other people? Is it living just as you will, turning your back resolutely on all convention, on all lies, and also on the co-operations of the old world? If that's it, could it be that you thought you were living out this dream in the life you've been leading over the past six months?'

'Oh no, certainly not! But the fact is I've still got too many sentimental attachments to my past life, I'm still too much of a student to set off for good, to become what I'd really like to be — a vagabond. Not the dismal, degraded vagrant that I am at the moment, but a vagabond ready to drink from every source of beauty, someone who travels through the vast universe radiant and free. It's this indecision, these regrets for the past which clash intolerably with the present, which have pushed me to the degradation I've told you about.'

'But if that's the case, why are you asking me what you should do? It's so simple! Make a resolution, an effort of will over yourself. I very much doubt whether, in your present moral state, you could take a proper decision. So get control over your actions again, go home and try with all your might, in all good faith and with all your energy, to make yourself into that student and man of action once again. If, without weakening or giving in, you find that your heart's no longer in it, that you can't stand that kind of life any more, leave it bravely, and go away to become a *bourlak* or vagabond, or anything you want to be. But don't let disorder take root in your life, don't let yourself simply drift. It's the surest way to endless misery and suffering.'

Orschanow had listened to Vera attentively. How right she was! It was so simple, salvation! He would do just as she said. And anyway, she was there: that would make everything easier.

'Thank you, Gouriewa, thank you! The only thing is, I shall need you for a long time to come yet.'

'I'll be here. Don't ever feel ashamed in front of me, don't ever think you could bore or exhaust me. In other words, don't think of me as a stranger. Now be careful not to overdo it, because that's also very dangerous. Makarow told me your room is very dark and dreary. You've only spent miserable days there recently. Go and find another room right now. Find one in the suburbs, clean and bright, above all bright. Then, make it agreeable to live in. Burn your *valet de cœur* rags and set to work. Whenever it's difficult or painful for you to do so, come here, day or night, whenever. As for friends, there's Makarow and Himmelschein. All the others could be morally harmful to you at the moment. A last piece of advice: stop your vagrant way of life right now, from today. Go for long walks, but not on Goutouyew or in Siennaya; go into the sun, out to the islands, into the countryside.'

Just as Orschanow was about to leave, old Anntone came in.

'Verotschka! you've been lecturing Orschanow . . . now why? After all, working for people's freedom, creating works of art, contemplating the splendours of the universe by the roadside, or praying to God from the sanctuary of a monastery all amounts to the same thing. Nothing matters, except the sincere and simple search for the right path.'

All his life Dmitri would remember the gentle old prophet's words. Vera started to laugh. 'Oh, Uncle, don't preach the contemplative life to Orschanow; he's got no need for it, he's already too much inclined in that direction!' She quite understood the broad-minded, liberal idea her uncle had expressed, but she also sensed something else.

Orschanow followed Vera's advice to the letter. He rented a bright, cheerful room. He set out some of the things he had brought back from Petchal. He put his books and notes in order. Yet in this attempt at resurrecting his previous life only one thing gave him real delight: his new-found friendship with Vera. This was enough to flood everything with sunshine, to put new life into him.

But Orschanow sincerely and naively attributed his sudden return to moral equanimity, and the serenity of the days which followed to the fact that he had made a resolution, that he had got himself out of the depths he had been in. From this point onwards he deluded himself more and more, until eventually he was living a complete daydream.

The attentive Vera, with her keen understanding of people's worth, however much it was hidden, rejoiced at the difficult and attractive task of getting Orschanow out of the morbid gloom into which he had sunk. This man was certainly not strong, but he wasn't vulgar or cowardly either. He was moody and changeable, but capable of feeling deeply. And the very intensity of his suffering, the extent of the moral misery he had fallen into, spoke of his high ideals and his thirst for beauty and purity. 'The darker the night, the closer to God.' Vera remembered this phrase, which she had found a long time ago in a biography of the great Dostoevsky, the poet of moral decay and human suffering.

6

Orschanow had completely given up frequenting the seediest parts of town, but there was one thing he regretted. He was aware of having abandoned poor Polia without a word of goodbye, and without even a few roubles to help her out a little. At Vera's request, the committee's fund had given him some money, and since he no longer felt irresistibly tempted by the areas where he and Polia used to meet, he resolved to go and find her one day and, on the pretext of going away, say goodbye and share the committee's money with her. He would do it in a few days' time, when he was quite sure of himself, and he would not mention the project to Vera for fear of worrying her.

He saw her every day, and each time he felt an inexpressible joy, an endless delight in hearing her speak, in watching her. She was so strong and tolerant, understanding and forgiving all weaknesses as long as people were struggling in good faith to overcome them. Her whole manner of speaking was appealing, her words full of imagery and her gestures confident and relaxed. Although she was serene, an air of gaiety softened the deep seriousness of her conscientious and upright nature. With her, Orschanow forgot all his anxieties and boredom.

Despite his sensual nature, Orschanow had a chaste respect for thinking and emancipated women, and a capacity for absolutely disinterested, pure friendship. The sense of gallantry, so poorly developed generally amongst true Russians, was absolutely lacking in him, as in all like-minded young men of his generation. To him, the woman who lived alongside him, sharing his work and his aspirations, was a human being, a distinct individual and not merely a member of the opposite sex. So he felt an entirely brotherly love for Vera, an affection mixed with gratitude. It did not occur to him that it could ever be otherwise, and that one day he might fall in love with her.

In other respects, Orschanow had calmed down. He spent much of his time alone in his room, working and using the holidays to make up for lost time. Sometimes he would go with Vera to old Anntone's house, and sometimes Makarow and Emilie would come too. Occasionally Rioumine would also be there, although his fanatical personality didn't appeal to Orschanow. Once, as a puny and nervous fifteen-year-old schoolboy, Rioumine had shot a high-ranking police officer in the middle of a holiday crowd. No one had seen him do it in the crush, or even suspected him, because of his youth. Since that time he had unfailingly risked his life or at least his liberty for the group's affairs, with rare *sangfroid* and unaffected self-sacrifice. His whole life was committed to the revolutionary cause, and he had no other *raison d'être*. A man like that could not understand a dreamer like Orschanow, with his vague and vast ideas, his love for an ideal of beauty.

Often Orschanow would bring his books to Vera's and they would work together, like the two students they were, with no troubling thoughts coming between them. The days slipped peacefully by for Dmitri, lit by Vera's presence.

*

One evening when he was on his own, Orschanow decided he was strong enough to make the melancholy pilgrimage out to Goutouyew and Polia. With no flicker of nostalgia, but rather with disgust, he went back to the squalid maze of little streets between the shabby wooden or brick houses. Some streets were lined with ugly and dilapidated factory buildings: candle factories, tanneries, paper factories, mills. Outside, new hides, crawling with worms, soaked in barrels, and bones and fetid rags lay around in heaps. The setting sun cast gold and purple lights onto the blurred reflections of stinking puddles.

Orschanow found Polia sitting on a beam near the factory where she worked. She had aged, her poor forlorn face had grown uglier, and premature wrinkles were etched around her slack eyes.

'Oh, Mitia! I thought you would never come back!'

'I was ill. Now I've found a job in the provinces, and I'm leaving tomorrow morning. I've come to say goodbye to you, Polia.'

'Oh . . . but if you're leaving tomorrow, you must at least spend the evening with me.'

'I can't. I have to get back. I've got some papers to see to. Goodbye, Polia, look after yourself, and adieu.'

'So you're going . . . just like that?' And tears started slowly rolling down Polia's already faded cheeks. Orschanow had not expected that, and it touched him to the quick. So Polia, the passive, unresponsive Polia, loved him!

It was true that, to her, Dmitri's departure meant the end of the pale ray of light which had lit up the grey shadow of her life for one brief moment. It had been something so rare and good to have a gentle lover like that, who did not beat her, ragged, buffeted and despised as she was. And now he was leaving!

'Mitia, Mitia! are you really going?'

Then, desperately, Orschanow took her in his arms, kissing her discoloured lips. He was crying too, stammering, 'Poor, poor Polia!' So, at this moment, the only person who loved him, apart from his strange and distant father, was the ragged Polia, so miserable, so crushed! The thought was sweet and infinitely sad to him.

'Come, Mitia, for the love of Christ, have mercy! Come with me just one last time, and we'll drink together and go to our place in the warehouse. Do you know, since you've been gone, I've often gone back there by myself. It's overgrown with grass now and a mountain ash has grown in the doorway. It's like a real room now.'

He followed her: why not do her a favour, give her a little alcohol and a little love, since this was the end, and since he would never be back.

They went into Arkhipour's bar. Some workmen there, who were already drunk, recognised Polia. They shouted out to her, teasing her good-naturedly: 'Hey, look, it's the tart! As soon as she's got a man, she starts on the brandy! Hey, gourd-face, you drink like a trooper!'

She turned her back on them, but gave as good as she got: 'What's it matter to you? You're not paying.'

They called back: 'Your sister's on the streets!'

'Now she's a beauty, is Lioubka!'

'Yes, not like this skinny nag!'

Dmitri, who was used to these scenes, interrupted calmly. 'Leave her alone, will you. I came here to have some fun, not to argue.'

The fat barman with a shiny, apoplectic face agreed: 'Come on, Mitrei Nikititch is right. Don't annoy people like that.'

Dmitri and Polia sat down at a table. A sudden acute anxiety clutched at Orschanow's heart: he had just drunk a large glass of brandy. Now he was going to get drunk, and then he was going to get trapped again! Just one moment of weakness had done it.

He took Polia outside, so as to stop drinking. Gently she pushed him towards the shadows of *their* warehouse. Suddenly, as Orschanow held Polia in his arms, something took hold of him and he crushed her in such a powerful embrace that she shuddered. He had been seized by an idea, a sudden vibrant image which had driven him mad, leaving him in such a shattered state of spent sensuality that he could scarcely think: he had imagined that, instead of the doleful Polia, he was holding Vera in his arms, possessing her. Once he had regathered his thoughts it suddenly seemed a sacrilege – in this place, in these surroundings, with this poor girl. He stood up, gave Polia half the money he had, and, kissing her on the forehead, left.

He fled without turning back, in spite of Polia's entreaties, taking with him through the dull, hot night the unbearable burning sensation, the fire which had so suddenly ignited, and which from now on nothing could extinguish.

He was almost running, for no good reason, since he was already far from Goutouyew. But he was spurred on by a fierce anger against himself. So, after all, he really was damned! If it wasn't his loafing, savage vagabond of a character which exiled him from human society, it was his senses which drove him mad and made him hideous in his own eyes!

What tortured him, what seemed monstrous, was the place and circumstances in which this passion for Vera had been kindled in him. How could it have happened? To be in Polia's arms, and suddenly to desire Vera, absolutely instinctively, with such a delirious frenzy that he thought he would die of it!

*

When he came in, Orschanow scarcely had the strength to light his lamp. He undressed, throwing his clothes haphazardly on the floor, and then lay down by the open window. In the warm air, sweet-smelling breezes wafted by, with the grassy smell of suburban gardens. The subdued light, pale as a convalescent's smile, slid over the pine parquet floor, onto the piles of open books and notebooks on the table. As he lay, Orschanow looked at the tops of the birches outlined in gold by the rising sun, and had the illusion of being back in the heart of the country.

For the first time since the nightmare of the previous night in Goutouyew, Orschanow calmed down, and felt a renewed happiness at being alive.

He had been working with a passion, as he did everything, and yet his studies failed to interest him any more.

He tried hard to believe in his vocation and sometimes managed to do so. But there was Vera ... Her image infiltrated the soft morning light flooding the room. She was the force of life. The radiance of her beauty was like a halo around her head, shining with the nobility of her thoughts. Dmitri almost idolised her, this woman he desired with his whole body. He found the burning sensation of this unfulfilled desire delicious, and gave himself up to it. Although he didn't realise it, it was because he would have preferred anything, even suffering, to the emptiness of his present life.

For a long time Orschanow stayed stretched out on his bed, savouring his feeling of languorous sensuality. When he got up, he felt renewed energy, almost gaiety, welling up inside him. For no apparent reason he was emerging from the blurred dreams of the past few weeks. He leant on the window-sill. The narrow gardens, divided by worm-eaten fences and etched with the black arabesques of mosses, were overgrown with straggly vegetation. Red hollyhocks flamed amongst the silky cups of violet morning glory, and huge sunflowers bent their brown, golden-haloed heads. A powerful scent came up from the plants and the moist, black earth in the wake of the humid night and the morning sun. Things were alive, things were looking sunny. And Orschanow loved life.

*

Towards evening Vera came in. As soon as she saw him, she realised he had changed since the previous evening, and it filled her with joy. Her senses were dormant, unawakened by her former marriage to Stoïlow. With her calm manner, all intellect, all action, Vera had come to think of herself as almost asexual. She felt a brotherly love for Orschanow, an affectionate concern. She had got used to having him near her almost the whole time, and to sharing his cares and worries.

'You're in tune with the weather today, Orschanow! You're looking sunny in the sunshine. What a change! Even yesterday you were so serious. What's caused this transformation — some happy news?'

'Oh no! You see, when I'm plunged into that state of moral depression you've seen me in for some time, a blind, unconscious battle rages inside me between life, health and this morbid numbness. Then suddenly one day, when sanity triumphs, I grow into my new skin again.'

Orschanow was watching Vera as she stood near the window. An intense and sweet feeling flooded through him, a reaching-out of his whole being towards her. But then something occurred to him, and saddened him.

'Listen, Gouriewa, it's you, it's your constant presence, it's the atmosphere of healthy rightmindedness you surround me with that's changing me. But these student friendships always end in a black moment, that of separation. And I can see that when that comes I'll sink back into lethargy and anxiety.'

He had spoken without knowing or noticing the impact of his words. Vera looked at him. Their eyes met, and Orschanow could no longer pretend. He took her hand and they stayed like that, silently, by the window looking out onto gardens which they no longer saw.

Vera had gone pale. She felt troubled. Her feelings were rebelling against their passive state and her virgin senses were awakening. For the first time she felt an immense desire to love.

41

7

Still they said nothing, in the delicious tension of the moment. Orschanow sensed that she was his, that she, too, was no longer the same, and an immense joy choked him. He took Vera's hands and held them to his chest. Vera, taking control of herself again, kept looking at him, with a soft, serious look, a promise. 'So be it,' she said finally. 'We'll carry on working and living alongside each other.' Yet she slowly pulled away from him. Orschanow was trembling, and his embrace had become violent, his lips pale. He suddenly pulled back, ashamed. Yet wasn't this happiness, wasn't she his, since she had promised? He didn't dare speak. He could find no words, nothing that wasn't banal, useless. And Vera left almost immediately, squeezing his hands with a smile and a caress in her look.

Orschanow fell on his knees near the window, his head in his hands. He felt an almost drunken sorrow. He was saved now, after all his despairing! And so easily, so simply.

*

In the road outside, Vera met Makarow. They had been close friends for years, frank and affectionate as man to man. So Vera poured out the new emotion which had come and overwhelmed her life.

'Gouriewa, I've watched you both, and I knew perfectly well it would come to this. But listen . . . I know Orschanow very well by now and I can tell you something in all conscience: if you want him to pass his doctorate, if you don't want him to fall back into lethargy, don't give in to him.'

They stopped in the deserted road. Vera listened to him attentively.

'Don't you think my influence and wishes will be enough?'

'No. Orschanow is a sensualist in everything he does. He lives for pleasure, in all its forms. He isn't always aware of it, but that's what is at the heart of his nature. All this frantic work he's been throwing himself into since he's known you has been for you, only for you. Tomorrow, if you're his, he'll give himself over entirely to his new passion, to sensuality, and no external force will make him flow against the tide. Believe me, Vera, don't do it. *When* he has passed his doctorate, then you must both go off, somewhere in the east, deep in the steppes.'

Vera realised that what Makarow said was true: in order to save Orschanow from himself, she had to find the strength to resist, to keep him in suspense.

8

At first Orschanow chafed at having to wait. Then, captivated, he began to savour the heady combination of melancholy and desire, and found a bitter-sweet pleasure in his very anxiety, in the ever-present yearning of his whole being for Vera.

*

The summer was drawing to a close, suffused with radiant sunshine. It was the holidays, and Orschanow scarcely went out at all any more, but kept staunchly at his work. Vera would often come in the evening, and they would walk around the sad suburban streets until late. They held hands, like two well-behaved children. Orschanow felt a few sudden quick awakenings of desire, atavistic urges from the almost savage feelings lying dormant within him. But Vera, very calm and firm, yet gentle, had the upper hand, and would not give in. Then he would fall back into his wistful, sensual reverie, glad at least to be spared suffering.

They said very little, just touching occasionally on the future, which seemed to them both full of hidden delights.

*

Then one day everything changed drastically. Orschanow received news from his brother Vassily of the death of their father, the old dreamer Nikita. And Vassily, whom Orschanow had not seen since he was small, asked him to come home to Petchal to try to sort out the muddle of the old man's affairs, to keep his name unblemished. The death of his father, whom he loved with a strange, aching love, left Orschanow feeling deeply bruised, and finally and definitively alone. Yes, he would go, he would make the mournful pilgrimage back to Petchal.

Vera let Orschanow go, thinking it would be a salutary rest for him after all the singlemindedness of the past few months. The day he was due to go, Orschanow felt ashamed not to feel as devastated as he surely ought to have done at leaving Vera. The idea that he was going off to see his father's grave struck him as very sad and touching, not at all desperate or gloomy.

44

As the Moscow train rattled across the flat, barren, sunlit country, Orschanow felt a sudden immense relief, almost a surge of joy, and it confused him. He tried not to look at the countryside, tried to resist the youthful high spirits which rose in him the further he left Petersburg behind. He was afraid of giving in entirely to these all-too familiar feelings: the longing for an *elsewhere*, the thrill of leaving. In the third-class carriage, the passengers changed at practically every station – peasants laden with bags and packets, smelling of sheepskin and tar, and women in gaudy *sarafanes*. A clutch of hens was clucking underneath a bench. A bold cock flapped its wings and started crowing. This brought a shriek of laughter from those in the carriage, a good-natured, spontaneous burst from these sociable people. Orschanow found himself joining in with them, wanting to find out about them. He despised himself enormously for feeling so high-spirited so quickly, when he had just left Vera and his work, and when he was on his way to Petchal, to see the ruins of everything he'd loved so much, to see his father buried, the house and garden sold. In the corner, some peasants started to sing: 'Don't you whisper, old mother oak grove! Don't stop the young lad following his fancy,' a ballad of long ago, from the marauding pirates of the steppes. To Orschanow it seemed an irresistible call to liberty, to the wandering life, to the vast, distant horizon.

Travelling through the silence of a countryside rustling with the first breath of autumn, the train rattled its way south-east, its proud, wild song slowly but surely taking Orschanow under its spell.

At the station Orschanow recognised their old servant Terennty, who ran up in tears, doffing his cap and kissing his master's son on the shoulder. Orschanow embraced the old man like a brother.

'Mitrei Nikititch! Who would have recognised you, if you didn't look exactly like our late master, Vladimir Nikolaitch!'

Then Orschanow noticed a tall, slim young man, with long, fair, silky hair and candid grey eyes coming up to him with outstretched arms. 'I'm your brother Vassily. We must get to know and love each other, Dmitri! There are only two of us now . . .' His voice broke and all three, the two brothers and the old servant, wept.

As they walked home through the narrow, empty streets of the town, Orschanow felt an intense pang of pleasure. Down below, in front of them, lay the broad, proud Volga, glistening with copper lights in the setting sun. Up on the hill the golden domes of the cathedral shone almost purple, and beyond them was the endless, flat horizon of the steppes.

'Oh, Vassina! Fancy seeing this again, after all these years, when so many changes have taken place in both our lives!'

'I know, Mitia. I never thought I'd feel such intense emotion in coming back to all the things I last saw as a child.'

They stopped for a moment when they reached the wooden gates to the house. The garden had become bushy and overgrown, and the trees were now giants, sheltering the pale tiled roof with their massive boughs. Autumn had scattered its rich layers of colour. The lime trees seemed covered with specks of gold, the pear trees flamed red with violet shadows, and the birches' green leaves were beginning to be dappled with yellow. Only the ancient oaks still kept their deep, dark green.

'Mitia, I've got good news for you,' Vassily said. 'Our father's old friend Bogdane Ostapow has bought everything – and he's not going to change it at all!' This was a great relief to Dmitri, who hated the idea of strangers tampering with this much-loved place. 'Yes, it's all arranged. And Ostapow has even promised to keep Terennty on.'

They went in. Nothing in the house had changed. All the familiar objects were there, now worn and old, but still in their usual places. Vassily and Dmitri walked through the house in silence. Dmitri found memories of the past flooding back, and Vassily respected the feelings of this brother whom he scarcely knew, but whom misfortune had now brought close. In fact, Vassily had followed Dmitri's progress through mutual friends in Petersburg, and already felt a great sympathy for this unusual individual, who seemed so similar to their father.

Terennty obstinately refused to sit down at his master's table, staying withdrawn and respectful.

'You see, Mitia, I could quite easily have managed affairs here without you . . . But I called you because I wanted to see you, and also because I thought you might need a rest. I know a lot about your life, and I assure you I was very worried about you, getting caught up in the misery and moral squalor of the slums. Poor Mitia! We couldn't help each other . . . I could have written, but I knew very well that it wouldn't help. Now that I hear Gouriewa is with you, I'm much happier. I met her in Moscow, and have the greatest respect and admiration for her. Stay close to her, let her guide you, and I can watch over you from a distance. For the moment, I'll do whatever's necessary here: as for you, just rest and go your own way as you will, and above all don't do any work!'

After he had been with his brother a little while, Orschanow was surprised to find him different from the way he had imagined him, as a cool, scientific sort, a strong but unromantic revolutionary, a little like Rioumine. He told him so.

'It's true, to most people I'm like that, but not towards you. After all, isn't there a mysterious blood tie between us, the tie of our common origins which nothing can erase or replace? I'll always be the same for you as you see me today. Always, whether near or far.'

Night was falling, and in the silence they could hear a light wind rustling the branches next to the house. They stayed up until very late, talking of their very different lives, trying to get closer to each other.

*

Each morning they would go down with Terennty to the cemetery at the bottom of the hill, where the steppes began. It was a modest patch of land studded with black crosses and surmounted by an old, lop-sided little wooden church, keeling over towards the earth, which was thick with human debris. It cast a gloom over this peaceful, forgotten corner, invaded by the almost tree-high grasses of the steppes.

The two brothers, both non-believers, knelt down, holding hands, next to the illiterate peasant who prayed and wept, crossing himself piously, and thought sadly of the kindly image of the dead man. These were good moments for Vassily and Dmitri, and deepened their growing affection for each other.

During the day, Vassily's time was taken up by an almost uninterrupted stream of creditors. Jews in sticky caftans, and greasy usurers with rolling eyes, done up in their new *poddiovkas*, hat in hand, respectful but dogged. All began by praising the dead man's virtues — a man of God, so gentle, so approachable, not arrogant. Then, shuffling their feet and scratching their necks, they would bring out a scrap of paper, some more or less fabricated bill.

Usually Vassily replied coldly: 'Wait until the house is sold, then I shall settle whatever accounts you can prove are genuine.'

But Terennty was incensed. He took the Russians to one side, refusing to have any truck with Jews: 'You haven't got the sign of the cross on you? Then you're wearing the seal of the Antichrist! Heartless cretins! You don't leave the master time to cool in his coffin, nor his sons time to mourn, before you fall on the house like a flock of crows on carrion! *May you rot in hell!*'

*

As autumn approached, and the purples and golds of the leaves deepened, Dmitri spent hours of immense contentment in the garden, lying on his back among the fine grasses and the scattered gold of the lime trees. Every day before dawn he would go down to the oak trees at the fringes of the steppes to watch the day breaking over the mist-covered plains. On the horizon, flaxen mists would swirl at ground level. Higher up there would be a blurred layer of sulphurous green. Higher still, the horizon turned from deep orange

49

to carmine; and then out of this vaporous world rose the deep, red, rayless sun. At that moment the mists cleared, and in the distance Dmitri could see low hillocks and scattered bushes, vague black spots on the blue background of the open steppes. This heady birth of the day above the seductive steppes filled Dmitri with a rush of joy, and his chest swelled with new vitality and force.

Yet his memories of Petersburg and of Vera still haunted him. He knew he would return, and take up his studies, and later marry Vera and become in her eyes a normal and productive man again. This was all well and good, but, apart from his love for Vera, it left him cold and indifferent. Yet there was no doubt that this was the way things would go, this was the future, the general formula. But behind this artificial horizon was another possible dawn, another guiding light, the love of the free, vagabond life, the love of the bewitching *elsewhere*. And Orschanow indulged himself, as in a venial sin, in fantasising over this dream, which he really believed was quite unrealisable: to set off one morning, poor and alone, to conquer the earth. To become a free vagabond sleeping on the side of the road, someone who possesses nothing and envies no one, someone at odds neither with himself nor with his fellow men, but happy in his independence, master of things, not dominated by them, and master above all of the infinite horizons. At such moments, Dmitri went so far as to imagine his goodbyes with Vera, and with Vassily, whom he had grown to love. These scenes would be the first step – sad, but very sweet – on the road to emancipation.

At other times his desire for Vera came back to torment him. He thought then that, if his dream were realised, it would mean abandoning Vera, and the loss of the hope which had kept him alive for months. And then he cursed himself and the alluring steppes. He would bury himself in the silence of the house, in his uncle Vladimir's empty apartment, and he would read, and work, and write to Vera. Yet still there was the sunlight, flooding in through the windows and casting a shifting green shadow from the huge nearby trees onto the pink pine of the fence.

Soon, in spite of his promise to Vera not to associate with such people any more, he went down to the river port and met up with his old friends the *bourlaki*. The fishermen and the local lads became his friends and companions. The passivity of the men pleased him, the unswerving force of their inertia under the relentless harshness of lives lived without hope. All their innate need for poetry, all their sorrows, all the suffering of their uncultivated souls and their hardened bodies – and, occasionally, something more male, a hint of revolt and daring – would be expressed in their songs, the marvellous songs which had totally captivated him when he was small.

He felt no flicker of guilt at the irresistible attraction which drew him once more into the simple, working-men's areas: these people, with their iron muscles and chests of bronze, working out in the open air, were nothing like the pale scraps of humanity from the slums of Petersburg. Admittedly they were poor, they drank, they sought quick, brutal love-making. After all, singing, drinking and coupling were their only joys. But they were healthy and laughing, and there was pure and energising air there, and good, beneficial sunshine.

In their company Orschanow forgot what was sad and iniquitous about the lives of the people he envied: the deserted villages where the women wore themselves out working the soil, pushing an archaic wooden plough, where children died in their hundreds from misery and illness, and where men did crushing work for pitiful wages – the perpetual slavery of the poor, the subjugated.

*

The autumn wind became colder, the twilights earlier. The beautiful multi-coloured foliage of the gardens littered the humid soil. A sadness, and a vague sense of serene agony, were abroad in the now often mist-filled air.

One day a storm raged through the steppes. The *perekati-polie*, that curious winter growth of the Slav deserts, rolled its little carbon balls along the ground. All night long the wind howled and sighed around the shaking house. By morning, the earth had taken on the winter shroud of snow it would wear for months to come.

'It's time for us to go,' Vassily said. 'Little Mitia, you've got your vigour and courage back. Now go back to your work, and I'll return to mine. In black times, always remember that you've got not only Gouriewa, but also a brother and a friend, more solidly built than you are for the hard fight our life must be if we are to be apostles and guides. Lean on me and don't worry, but don't become hardened and insensitive. Always remember the example of generosity and kindness that our father set us.'

*

In Moscow the two brothers parted company. As they embraced for the last time, both suddenly wept. And Dmitri had a clear sense that never again would he see this brother who had come into his life so suddenly, and the flash of intuition filled him with gloom. He was longing to see Vera again, but then there was Petersburg, which he now hated, and *work*. All this caused him an intense unease, a dumb irritation.

The train rolled on with a flat, suffocated sound over the endless, snow-covered plains. The full, heavy sky seemed to weigh low on this immense desolation. How little this return journey resembled the outward trip, which had been full of the excitement of coming towards liberty and rest in the silence of the steppes.

*

Vera, Makarow and Emilie were waiting for Orschanow. He seemed to have grown, and he looked so robust, with his suntanned face and neck, and his brown hair falling with careless grace across his broad forehead.

At first it was enchanting for Dmitri to see Vera again. For the first time he held her in his arms, kissing her on the lips like a lover. Vera, a little surprised by his new manner, was covered in uncharacteristic confusion. Orschanow was exuberant and high-spirited, full of the happiness of the moment. But abruptly, as they walked back to their suburb, everything changed. When Vera spoke, in all innocence, Dmitri was suddenly reminded of all his doubts and apprehensions.

'Now that you're strong and healthy you can get back to work again. This winter, you'll have to work particularly hard.'

This reminder of everything he had come to dread since his time in Petchal drove him to dumb anger, and he refused to reply, clenching his teeth and mentally cursing the blind fanaticism of these people, the slavery they imposed on others, and which he suspected them of wanting to impose

53

on him. And for a few seconds he hated Vera, with all his unappeased desire, and with all his need for liberty too. Vera went pale, sensing that he had slipped away from her again, this time perhaps forever. She reproached herself bitterly for having let him leave, for having stupidly encouraged his trip. She was in silent agony, as an abyss seemed to open up between them. She decided to try to prove to Orschanow how unjust he was being, and she came and took his head, and kissed him.

'Mitia, if you believe everything that anger is telling you, you're wrong. I'm yours, whatever you may be. I'd rather sacrifice everything I've dreamt about for us than feel that you hate me.'

Orschanow pulled her towards him and they stayed like that without speaking. It was a bitter, unfathomable moment. Then it suddenly occurred to Orschanow that, if he accepted Vera's sacrifice, it would shackle him to her forever, that he would never be strong enough to reclaim his liberty, and that their whole life would consist of the mortal and rebellious boredom which had come on the heels of his return. A boundless ordeal was about to open up before them.

IO

The days went by, drab and monotonous. Orschanow was on a downhill slope, and he didn't even try to check himself. He worked listlessly, prodded occasionally into a fit of furious and exasperated endeavour when Vera preached at him. The growing violence of his undisciplined nature frightened Vera as she began to realise her inability to deal with it. But time was short, and the examinations were looming. She tried to get Orschanow down to serious work again, chivvying him gently: if he didn't pass, what would he do afterwards? She made the mistake of adding that the committee's aid fund would not help him any more if he hadn't really applied himself. Orschanow replied curtly that he had no need of help, that he wouldn't basely sell his freedom for a living. He would become a labourer, a vagabond, anything, but never a slave.

Then he threw himself miserably onto his bed, wrung his hands in rage and misery and reproached Vera for what he called her insensivity.

'Oh, Vera, Vera! Why do you torment me like this? It's not me you love, it's an idea, a formula! You promise to be mine, then you torture me for months on end. You use my passion to serve your evangelical zeal. You're thoughtless and cruel!'

He pushed her away brusquely and left without another word, without even a goodbye.

Alarmed, Vera got up and called after him, but Orschanow ignored her and ran on through the streets, much to the astonishment of the passers-by, who turned and stared. Vera took her coat and left the house, shaking. She must find him at all costs. One thought obsessed her: she mustn't lose him, she must see him again and get him back. But where had he gone? Then she remembered his previous haunts, and his weakness for Siennaya and Goutouyew Island. She strode along, oblivious to the intense cold. Night was falling and she nearly got lost in the little streets, which she hardly knew.

Just as she was beginning to lose heart, a terrible thought made her break into a run. She pictured Orschanow hurling himself into one of the holes bored in the ice of the canals or the Neva. It was dark by the time she came to Goutou-yew, the thick, drab dark of the thaw, and she stopped, overcome with mortal tiredness. Where could she find Dmitri in this maze of factories, waste land, depots, in all this swarming misery where she had never been before, and knew no one? Was she going mad? How had she, usually so energetic and calm, got into this state of moral disarray? Why hadn't she even thought of calling Makarow, and getting him to help her find Orschanow? Yet here she was, so for a while she just walked around, trusting to luck, hoping for a chance encounter.

All of a sudden she stopped, and everything reeled in front of her: a bar door had opened and through the grey pipe smoke she had glimpsed Orschanow slumped over a grimy table at the back of the room, with a bedraggled girl running her rough working hands through his hair, trying to rouse him. As if in a trance, Vera went in, walked up to Orschanow and shook his arm.

'Get up, Dmitri.'

Orschanow had already had enough time to drink a great deal of brandy. He was bleary-eyed, and his face was deathly pale. Vera saw a look of horrified dismay on his face. But he got up and followed her, docilely, without a murmur, not looking at anyone, stumbling against the benches. When Vera had first come in, everyone had fallen silent. The barman and customers had stared, stupefied, but then they had broken out laughing at this unusual scene. Seeing Orschanow going towards the door, the barman called out: 'Hey, Mitrei Nikititch! What about the money?' Orschanow didn't hear him and went out, and it was Vera who had to pay, much to the raucous amusement of the rest of the room.

Polia was also very drunk, and had got up when she saw Orschanow go. Now she accosted Vera in dull indignation.

'What are you doing here, lady? You just come in and pinch other people's men, just because you've got better clothes! With a dress like yours, you would've thought you'd be ashamed to come into bars like this. It's all right for us, of course, we're just the dregs!'

Outside, Orschanow had collapsed on a pile of stones in the snow. He could only understand one thing through his drunken haze: Vera had suddenly appeared in old man Arkhipour's bar, in Goutouyew. In the name of God, how on earth had that happened?

'Get up, you idiot!' Vera ordered him harshly, seeing that he was drunk, and afraid he might not follow her if she seemed to relent. He obeyed again, and followed her meekly as she led him by the hand. She walked without knowing where she was going, trying to find her way by the flickering light of a few red gas lamps in the dingy maze of the island. In the dismal silence forlorn songs drifted out of bars, and drops of water dripped from the rooftops with the rhythm of rain.

Suddenly they came upon an empty black space in front of them: it was the sea, which meant they had crossed the island, leaving the town behind them. Orschanow's strength was failing him and, dazed and reeling, he finally fell down in the snow, unable to get up. His head rolled from side to side and he was stammering incoherently. Vera took him in her strong arms, lay him down on some dryish beams, took off her coat and draped it over him. She sat down next to him and mechanically rolled a cigarette.

The thaw continued, with long cracking sounds, the noise

57

of breaking crystal, as the ice broke up in the canals and pools. A heavy mist was hanging over the sea in the darkness, making the air milder. Vera waited, utterly exhausted by her defeat. It was all over now, she couldn't have any more illusions. After all that she had hoped to inspire in him, here was Orschanow, drunk, unconscious. And this was the way it would always be.

On top of this she, Vera, hadn't got the strength to take up her own life where she had left off, leaving Orschanow to carry on alone on his miserable route. And she despised herself for being so weak: she hadn't managed to change him and make him her own. Now she would have to subjugate herself to him.

*

The awakening was grim, in the grey light of dawn. Instantly Orschanow remembered everything clearly, and wondered once again how Vera had managed to find him in Arkhipour's bar. But he said nothing, tormented by unspeakable remorse and shame. He stood up, avoiding Vera's eyes. She saw his suffering, and did not reproach him. What was the use, since everything was over?

The two of them walked without a word through the wretched squalor of the island, which was just waking up to its misery after the oblivion of the night, and on through the empty streets of Petersburg. But Orschanow was thinking, trying to combat the depression flooding through his whole being and paralysing his will: a resolution had to be made. Why was he following Vera again? Where was this leading him? He ought to stop right here and now, shake hands and say goodbye.

Yet still he kept on walking, afraid to make the move.

58

With mounting despondency, he found himself back in the courtyard to his house. 'Go on up!' Vera ordered, as he stopped. He climbed the stairs slowly and painfully, and a sudden shiver ran down his spine. His limbs felt heavy, and he leant against the window in misery, wishing Vera would go and leave him alone. All at once everything pitched and tossed before his eyes and he fell. Once again Vera picked him up, laying him on his bed and helping him take off his wet clothes. Then Orschanow fell into a kind of delirium.

Vera stayed with him, calm and resigned to the inevitable. What did all this degeneration, all this misery, even all this weakness matter! She would stay with Dmitri, she would look after him throughout their lives, just as she had last night.

*

For eight days Orschanow was in the grip of fever and delirium. Towards evening he would wake up, open his eyes and see Vera's svelte, blue-clad silhouette going to and fro in the glow of sunset. Then he would close his eyes again and pretend to be asleep, so that he didn't have to talk. What could he have said to her? And why was she still there, in spite of everything?

He didn't speak because he couldn't find the courage to tell her the truth: he wasn't going to work any more, he was going to drop his studies and become a labourer and vagabond. He renounced everything she'd dreamed of for him and for herself. And yet he still wanted her, and wanted to make her his.

Makarow and Emilie called in every evening. Orschanow neither liked nor disliked them. Still, knowing Makarow,

59

he was counting on him to tell Vera what he himself would certainly never have the strength to tell her.

As the days went by Orschanow began to feel himself coming back to life again. One pale April morning his life force returned. It was so warm that Vera had opened the window wide. The sun was pouring in, making playful arabesques on the white pine floor and over the red silk bedspread. Vera was reading with her back turned to Orschanow, which was a relief to him. He awoke feeling quite different, sensing a new life coursing through his limbs. How warm it was, and how good that felt! He sat up quietly so that he could savour the pleasure of the moment alone. Why had he distrusted life so much, why had he tortured himself so? He looked at things now in a different, reconciled light. Vera . . . Yes, she was there, in all her disturbing beauty; in this light her hair seemed more black and velvety than before, and he traced a purer, fuller line from her shoulders to her hips underneath her dark dress.

And he wanted her. But wasn't she just a part of everything that was attractive about the day, everything that was basking in the sunshine? Orschanow fell back onto the white cushions. He was seized with a sharp, burning sensation: he was coming back to life, and finding her beautiful again. But since there was an abyss between him and Vera, shouldn't he keep quiet, hide his happiness, and just *leave*?

*

Orschanow deliberately prolonged his convalescence, out of cowardly indolence, saying he felt weak and tired whenever Vera asked him. Once he admitted to being better and strong enough to go out, shouldn't he then put an end to it all with one word, and go forever? But in the meantime he gave himself up to the pleasure of his recovery and to the bitter-sweet sensation of desiring Vera, who was so near and so far away.

Vera was glad to see him almost well again, and to see the occasional smile on his lips and in his eyes. His silence she attributed only to shame and remorse, as he replied quietly and briefly to her questions, never talking about himself.

And Orschanow told himself that he could afford to enjoy these last days with Vera, sad but, for him, sweet days: afterwards, he would resolutely say goodbye to her and go elsewhere, anywhere, to meet his destiny. But meanwhile, why hurry?

II

It was while he was in this state of listlessness that Orschanow was overtaken by an unexpected turn of events, which tied him more closely to Vera for several months.

One night, just as he had sunk into sleep after reading his favourite poet, Vera woke him abruptly. In a steady voice, she told him to get dressed at once.

'One of our group has informed against us, and now the police are after us all. Come quickly.'

Orschanow hesitated. What did it matter if he got hard labour? Wasn't he going to be in bondage to *them* anyway, particularly to Vera, perhaps forever?

'But . . . I don't want to leave.'

Vera gestured impatiently. 'Come at once, or I'll stay here.'

Outside it was raining, and the night was humid and dark. In the silence they could hear the patter of rain on the roofs and the deserted pavements. In a neighbouring house, a lamp burnt muzzily, its light filtered through the pink curtain. Vera took short-cuts through gardens, jumping over fences and hedges, slipping in the mud.

'But where are we going?'

Orschanow cursed himself for having been such a coward as to give in to the luxury of convalescence. Now, he would have to go to ground somewhere with Vera and the others, and, at the very least, share their lives for months. Vera replied without stopping: 'Makarow is waiting for us in the country not far from here, at the house of his mistress's mother, an old peasant woman. Luckily I know where it is.'

'But why didn't they arrest us all at the same time?'

'When I came back at about eleven, I found Prokhor, our gardener, waiting to intercept me on the road. "Leave at once, Vera Nikolaïewna," he said, "the police are at your house. The master says you're to leave and not to worry about him, because it's not him they're after. He will send money on to you through M. Rioumine." And that's all. I ran to Makarow's straight away, and Emilie was there. She went off separately, and I came to you. That's all I know.'

Who had betrayed the committee? And why hadn't the police managed to capture them all? Orschanow angrily dismissed the questions besieging him: what did all that matter? As far as he was concerned, all this was a cruel irony: to be persecuted for a cause he no longer served or believed in!

Meanwhile, as they ran, Vera was saying: 'Don't worry, it won't be too bad at all where we're going: Makarow's woman is a serf's daughter, living alone with her widowed mother in the middle of a huge park, in a house their masters left them when they went to live abroad. We'll be in the depths of the country, quite safe and sound. You'll be able to rest, and recuperate.'

Orschanow, almost hating Vera at that moment, felt like laughing sarcastically. What right had she to want to keep a hold on him like this, regardless of his feelings? No, no, she wouldn't succeed: as soon as he could he would leave on his own, whatever the dangers. Oh, to be alone, alone and free!

12

In the silence of their retreat, ministered to by the two solicitous peasants, Vera and Makarow took up their studies again, resolutely undistracted by the events which had disrupted their peace and brought a temporary end to their mission. Orschanow kept a fierce, silent distance from them, spending hours stretched out on his bed or leaning on the window-sill. He wasn't dreaming, he was *waiting*.

The widow Domna Vassiliewna, a small alert woman in black, served their cause with quiet energy. It was through her that they had been put back in touch with Rioumine, who was working incognito in a factory. Every week she brought instructions from him. His advice to them was to stay where they were for a while. Orschanow felt that Rioumine was right. The police would begin to think they had gone abroad, and relax their surveillance. But he might not wait as long as the others. Sadly, but without the will to fight it, he recognised that everything that was good and kind in him had gone numb, and what had taken its place was a bitter determination to live a free and solitary life. In an effort to avoid painful explanations, he never spoke of the future. But he felt Makarow's soul-searching eyes scrutinising him, and it made him feel awkward and frustrated.

Makarow and Vera often spoke about Orschanow. Vera thought they should leave him alone and not press him, but Makarow reckoned it would make no difference to his state of mind.

'As long as he was trying to find his way through suffering, and was battling against that indisciplined, indulgent side of himself which has taken him over now, I liked Orschanow,' Makarow said one day. 'But he has really changed, and I don't expect much of him any more.' However, Vera loved him, and wanted to hope; and yet it was just Vera's obstinate determination to believe he could return to his previous life which most exasperated Orschanow.

The stay with the two peasant women dragged on, and Orschanow began to doubt Rioumine's judgement. He had an idea of his own: to get in touch with one of the Finns who owned sailing-boats in the Baltic, and to pay him to take them to some Scandinavian or German port. One day, without telling his companions, he got Domna Vassiliewna to convey his escape plan to Rioumine, suggesting he would find the Finns in a certain low bar in Goutouyew. Soon everything was fixed.

In May a large boat called the *Maria* was due to make two journeys to the German coast. The fugitives would split into two groups and go with her. Orschanow, Vera

64

and Makarow would make up one group; Rioumine, Emilie and Garchina the second. They drew lots for the first group to go . . . and fate decided Orschanow.

There was still another month to wait – a long time, but at least the departure date was fixed. The painful uncertainty Orschanow had been living in was over, and his peace of mind returned. But he still avoided the others, not wanting to encourage either the illusions which Vera entertained about him, or the confrontations he dreaded. He felt a pang of anguish at the idea of leaving Russia forever. His dream of being a Russian vagabond was never to be! Then, there was Vassily. He had to leave without saying goodbye to him, without even writing, in case he compromised him. Yet in another way leaving was a deliverance, the end of agonising doubts and hesitations.

*

The date of departure drew nearer. From the German port the *Maria* would take them to, the fugitives would go on to Geneva, and carry on their revolutionary action there. What would Orschanow do, Vera worried anxiously, once he was free again, and more removed from her influence? Would he even stay with them? Since he still refused to say anything on the subject, Vera thought it was up to her to try to get close to him, rather than leaving him alone with his thoughts, which, she sensed, only detached him more and more from her and his companions.

She decided to go to see him in his room one evening. His small, simple room, with a desk which had obviously not been used for a long time, and a narrow, red and white schoolboy's bed, was feebly lit by a red-shaded lamp. The fresh, humid air of the park, scented with pine and birch, came through the open window in gusts. Orschanow was sitting on the edge of his bed, his head between his hands, brooding. Vera's arrival was a welcome distraction, and he greeted her with relief. She stood in front of him, smiling, holding his hand in hers.

'Since you've been so naughty and so gruff, trying to avoid me all the time, then I suppose I have to come to you.'

'If you like. Only I don't want talk about it, it'll only make me uncomfortable. Anyway, what's the point of talking about the future, since we can't decide anything, and since we're stuck here? I wish you'd learn to enjoy the present moment, Vera, and simply give in to it, over and above everything else, anywhere and at any time!'

'But what's the point if it only lasts an instant, and plunges us into a black abyss afterwards?'

'It's very wrong of you to say that. What you're asking for, Vera, what you're always striving for, is the absolute – which is to say the impossible! You're asking life for what it cannot give – and that's a sure path to disillusion and suffering.'

'So, according to you we have to live from day to day, snatching the pleasure of the moment, without any thought for tomorrow?'

'Perhaps.'

'Well then, let's do that: we'll let tomorrow come without thinking about it. Everything passes, and who knows, perhaps one day we'll find each other again.'

But Orschanow wasn't listening any more. His chest felt heavy, and he was suddenly overwhelmed by desire. As he pulled the unwilling Vera towards him, his words came out in a jumble.

'Oh Vera, darling Vera! Why wait until later for happiness? You don't know ... You don't know anything! You're naive, like a child, so white, so pure. Tomorrow, no one knows what'll become of us ...'

Instinctively, Vera struggled, but her head was spinning in a whirl of unfocused thoughts, and her body quivered, finally aroused. Orschanow pressed Vera's lips forcibly against his. They were both trembling and unsteady; and now Vera abandoned herself to his ardour, as he seemed to want to crush her in his arms.

Orschanow held her for a long time, flesh against flesh, savouring the overflow of their happiness. He felt pride, but also a new kind of pleasure, slower, deeper, in having her there, so sweet, and in looking deeply into her eyes, full of tenderness and mystery. Vera looked at him wordlessly, inert ... But at length her look began to disconcert him.

'How different you are!' he said at last, shivering.

He drew away a little to admire the red glow of the lamp on Vera's pale skin, against the faded red silk of the bedspread. He played with her black curls, and bit her lips, which had grown paler. Still Vera said nothing.

'Speak to me! You frighten me like that!'

Almost fiercely, she took him into her supple arms again, as strength began to come back to her.

'Be quiet! Be quiet! There's nothing more to be said.'

*

As darkness fell, Makarow returned to the house after a fretful walk in the park. Domna and her daughter were sitting at the round table, sewing in silence, engrossed, their eyes down, as the samovar's doleful lament petered out.

'Where's Vera?'

Domna lifted her head, looking like a pale Byzantine nun.

'Vera Nikolaïewna has gone to Dmitri Nikititch's.'

'Has she been away long?'

'Quite a while.'

It was eleven o'clock. Makarow said nothing. Leaning against the window he saw the sleeping park, and sensed its powerful breathing rising in the milder air. A dull malaise flooded through him. He closed his eyes, and a vision came to him which cut him to the quick: Orschanow, Vera . . . he despised himself for it.

'Damnation! Is it anything to do with me? She'll get hurt, yes! But that makes me no less of a pig. I've been pricked by something, some unknown night beast . . . yes, yes, a brutish jealousy!' He spat and walked away from the window. Taking up his books and notes, he set to work with nervous energy.

*

Orschanow and Vera did not try to hide their feelings. Although they were quiet the next morning, their faces radiated an inner joy, and they didn't leave each other for a second. Orschanow in particular had changed, looking younger and more vital, standing taller, his head held high, his eyes bright again. For the first time since they had arrived he chatted and laughed, improvising teasing songs about the *Maria*, his 'lover', who was being slow in coming to pick him up.

Vera watched him happily. She was learning from him how to give herself up to the joy of the fleeting moment

68

and not to think of a tomorrow which, for them, did not exist. But, caught up in the full, intoxicating flow of their illusions, neither of them knew that yet.

PART TWO

I

Drab mists above the colourless sea-swell, great winds howling over the sad Baltic. A smoky port, mighty docks, a steely, strong outline beneath an unremitting grey sky. Then plain upon plain, sandy or fertile. And finally the high mountains and romantic valleys of central Germany.

In Geneva, spring had arrived. Skirted by distant mountains, the city lay gravely, but not morosely, in its valley, reflected calmly in the lake and the deep waters of the Rhône. It was pretty: pleasantly trimmed with its finery of chestnut and plane trees, neat and clean, its *coquetterie* discreet, without gaudiness or noticeable gaiety. Along the banks of the fast-flowing, muddy Arve, at the foot of Champel Hill and the Roseraie, lay the haunt of students, Plainpalais. Here a whole young Russia was lodged, bruised but full of life. Here, far from the shadows and horrors, out in the open sunlight, daring, fervent revolutionary hopes blossomed freely. There were stormy meetings, noisy clubs, overflowing passions, and, above all, youthful sincerity.

From the first, Vera and Makarow had breathed the air of this benevolent atmosphere with a glow of relief after their setbacks in Russia. With her senses appeased by the new delights of love, Vera's fighting instinct returned, as she set about making a new life for herself, getting down to work, and recovering her peace of mind.

Orschanow gave himself up completely to the joys of the open air and the sun, exhilarated by all the new things around him. He would go out of town at dawn, as he used to in Petchal, and wander randomly through the fields, amongst the crops shimmering in the light wind, along the blossom-studded hedges full of a life of their own, or in the oak woods tangled with undergrowth.

At other times he went out to explore the town alone, instinctively ferreting out the districts of particular beauty and stillness. He found the old part of Geneva, Calvin's town, with the great St Pierre Cathedral, which iconoclastic Protestantism had deprived of its treasures, but whose robust, mellow russet walls still seemed suffused with all the dark, evocative dreams of centuries; and in amongst silent, narrow, dead lanes, he found the bishop's palace, now a prison, so old that its red walls harboured a thick moss of humid green.

One day Orschanow had his first taste of the south. It was in the rue des Corps-Saints. Drops of sunlight fell on the blackish pavement and onto the dark old houses, giving them warm brown and golden tones. There were matt reds and greenish blues, canary yellows jostling with pale pinks and all the ugliness of black or grey had disappeared.

*

Orschanow was still not working, but was giving himself over entirely to the delights of wandering days and passionate nights, in which he tyrannically stifled Vera's reproaches with his caresses. Through possessing her, a certain pride and jealousy had grown inside him, so that when he saw her giving a part of her love to the student life which he now hated, he felt resentful. Sometimes, if she came back late from a meeting, he would wait for her in a fevered torment. Yet if she asked him to come along too, he refused fiercely. Only days of solitude, silence and peaceful, sensuous enjoyment calmed him down again, giving him real delight.

Curiously, since possessing Vera he had found that he felt free, instead of feeling the slavery he had expected and dreaded. Gradually the desire grew in him once more to set off and become the proud vagabond, out to conquer new horizons. He started to imagine all the bitter-sweet delight of leaving and abandoning Vera. She wouldn't die of it: she would find somewhere to live, and new things to give her pleasure. He luxuriated in his fantasy.

The inevitable finale was precipitated by the others, and by Vera herself. They pressed and cajoled him to rejoin their group, trying to trap him, to tie him down again. One evening they were all together in Vera's room. Vera, pale-faced and anxious, was looking at him, her eyes veiled with reproach.

'Could it possibly be that you're a coward, Dmitri? You ought to be working, and fighting, and being a man. I can't believe you're a coward – so tomorrow you really must go and register at the university and start work.'

Orschanow got up.

'A coward? No, that's what you all are. You're trying to set up liberty for a thousand years from now, a doubtful liberty at that, and yet you haven't the courage to take society, imbecile, deadening and judgemental as it is, by the throat and shake it up right now! A coward you say, Vera – the man who made you his, who made something of his soul vibrate in the very quick of your flesh! All right, so be it. I'll disappear, I'll go. But you'll stay mine, Vera, and nothing will take me away from you, ever. Now leave me! Leave me alone!'

He went over to the window and leaned his forehead against the pane, in turmoil. An overwhelming rebellion was seething in him. He heard Garchina say, 'If he'd left when he first threatened to, he'd already have travelled a long way!' Orschanow shrugged his shoulders in fury.

When the others had gone, Vera tried to pacify him. He took hold of her and pushed her towards the bed. She resisted, and fought back. Orschanow was blinded by anger and desire as their bodies writhed together in a fierce fight.

'You brute! You coward!' groaned Vera, her face pale, a hard line etched between her eyebrows. Soon they fell onto the floor. Orschanow's cruel and brutal coupling filled Vera with shame and disgust.

He got up. At his hands, Vera's right wrist had started to bleed. She was pale and hadn't responded to his embraces; and she bitterly resented him for it.

Something had been shattered.

She left the room without saying a word.

Orschanow flung himself onto the bed and banished all memory of what had happened from his thoughts, in an overriding need to calm himself.

The next day, chastened, he went and knelt in front of Vera, who was sitting in her room reading. Taking her hand, he suddenly noticed the wound he had given her the previous evening, and wept with self-reproach.

'Poor, poor Mitia,' she said with wistful tenderness. 'You'll never be one of us now.'

'You know I love you.'

'But your love is like everything about you; tormented, crazy. And yet, I'm so fond of you! Let's stay here close to one another, don't let's say anything, don't let's hope for anything.'

The rest of the day slipped by in a deep, subdued sadness. The pink light of evening dusted the promenade's golden

trees and the room's white walls. Vera went out. Orschanow felt a great, assuaging peace descend on him.

*

Through the open window, the blue light of dawn fell onto
the parquet floor. In the heavy silence of the suburb, several
cockerels crowed a premature awakening, and workmen's
clogs began to clatter on the pavement outside.

Orschanow woke with a start, knowing that he had
something important to do that morning. Now he remembered. It was all over. He was going to leave. His heart
contracted a little for a second. Then he leapt up, ready to
sing for joy. But as he dressed, putting on his old Petersburg
clothes, he calmed down, and gradually regained his mood
of the previous evening. He scribbled a few simple, sincere
words of affection and farewell to Vera, and then he left.

The sun was only just rising behind the lacy peaks of the
Voiron Mountains. Everything was bathed in an opal light,
and a gentle breeze passed though the branches of the trees,
shaking out a fresh, light shower of dew.

Orschanow took the white Savoy road, which led off
between green fields towards the softly undulating hills of
Mont-de-Sion. The day was clear and brimful of beauty,
and he strode out, feeling long-forgotten reserves of energy
and life rising in him. With his body's strength and suppleness in harmony with this inner joy, he felt capable of
walking forever, in his quest for the world and its most
far-flung horizons.

So that was it. He had had the courage to leave everything, even Vera, and to set off, a free man. In this frame
of mind, Orschanow went off in the sunshine of the May
morning.

2

At the top of Copponex Hill a huge old oak twisted its sturdy, thick-budded arms. Up against its solid trunk a wild apple tree grew, its branches stretching across the road, laden with white, scarlet-splashed blossoms. Below, lemon-yellow primroses and carmine anemones were scattered brightly on the dark velvet of the moss, and a little further on was a spiky hedge of white-flowering mountain blackthorn. Etched against the plain at the end of the field was the heavy silhouette of an old Savoy farm, square, low, half-buried in the ground, and covered in flat tiles blackened by time. A column of blue smoke rose from it into the soft, tranquil evening air. It was the end of spring, and a strong breath of life and fruitfulness mingled with the smell of the impoverished dwelling, which reeked of stables and rancid fried onions.

Orschanow, wearing a smock and carrying a bundle tied to the end of a stick, walked along unhurriedly, enjoying the calm of the evening and the simple landscape. He had walked like this through Savoy for two months, from hamlet to hamlet, from farm to farm. From his time in Russia he had learnt many small skills from the workmen he enjoyed mixing with: wheelwrights, blacksmiths, carpenters. And anyway it was so easy, in this primitive countryside, among the Savoy peasants: you asked for soup and a bed in exchange for a helping hand or some small repair job.

The painful memories of the past few months were fading for him. It all seemed so far away now, knowing that he would never see Vera again, that it was all over. He hadn't forgotten her, and the figure he had loved often came to him in dreams, veiled with melancholy. But instead of feeling sorrow or regret, Orschanow enjoyed the delicious glow of renunciation.

Oh, to be alone, to be free, unknown, with no ties or attachments, treading the traveller's welcoming, soft earth! To fall asleep in some chance spot, possessing nothing, attached to nothing, and the next day to travel on into different surroundings, amongst other people . . . and so on forever! It was at twilight above all, his favourite hour, that Orschanow savoured all the things whose melancholy sweetness he had instinctively sensed for so long, and whose appeal had finally seduced him.

He walked up to the farm. In the courtyard an old woman in a blue apron and white bonnet was sitting on the mossy doorstep peeling vegetables. Orschanow greeted her, and asked if there was any work to be had. The old woman fixed him with a stare.

'And where might you've come from?'

'From Sergy, where I did some repairs for M. Mouchet, the Count's farmer.'

'Ah, well . . . So you're looking for some work?'

'That's it, my good woman.'

'Well, it all depends if it's a matter of taking you on, or just a matter of a bed, seeing as how there's no vacancy, it being the wrong time of year. At haymaking, it'd be a different matter, but now, there's nothing. As for a bed, I don't rightly know. Perhaps. Trouble is, we've got one extra already, a traveller . . . so with you, that'd be two. Still, from here to Bozon's farm is four miles – quite a way. Well, if you want to sleep here, you could chop the wood and stack it. The other fellow's gone to help my husband cut grass for the cows. All right then, there'll be a pot of soup for you. If there's enough for four, there's enough for five.'

Orschanow set down his bundle. A tall blonde girl, robust as a man, with a serious, unsmiling face gave him an axe and showed him a pile of oak roots.

'There you are. When you've finished, put it there, in the shed behind the hay rick.' The two women got on with their work, occasionally exchanging remarks in patois, but paying no attention to him as he cut the hard, knotty wood only a few feet away from them.

*

Inside was a square room, with hams and strings of dried onions hanging from broad, smoke-stained beams. On the blackened walls were shelves stacked with old earthenware pots, and old-fashioned utensils were ranged above the huge chimney. In the clear flames of the twine-fire a great melting-pot hung suspended from an antique iron trammel, a vestige of a forgotten nomadic life. On the table were a petrol lamp, conical bowls of soup, their rough enamel patterned with red and green, and an enormous ten-pound cob loaf.

The large-boned men sat heavily on benches polished with use, their muscles solid under their fustian smocks and trousers. None of them had taken off their hats. The women served them, their sleeves rolled up.

The farmer, an old peasant with a wizened, shaved face, poured wine into the thick glasses. The other vagabond, a thickset man with frank blue eyes and a blonde moustache growing over a good, firm mouth, seemed ill at ease. So the farmer said, in his country drawl, 'Now then, you lot, you mustn't be ashamed. If we offer soup, it's willingly we do it. Better to ask than to steal, isn't it now? After all, it can happen to any man, not to find work. Now's not the season for idlers, that'll be when there's most work around. Come on and drink with us then, and show us you're no more of a darned fool than the rest of us!'

Ever since setting out from Geneva, Orschanow had observed with curiosity these people of a different race, people without the resigned melancholy and vague mysticism of the Russian peasant, who worked less and contemplated life more.

'It's work, iniquitous, endless work which has made them like this,' he thought. 'They're like labouring beasts, they don't have the time to lift their heads and look around them at the wide horizons, or to breathe freely the air which belongs to everyone. Yes, it's sedentary life, property, family, work, everything that makes up society which is brutalising and destroying them, dragging them down towards the soil in a bitter hourly struggle, hardening them, making them ugly.'

*

As they lay side by side on the soft sheaves in the dusty hay loft the travellers talked together. They told what they chose to tell of their past lives, Orschanow, hiding his intellectual past, calling himself an émigré Russian worker.

Antoine Perrin came from Bugey. While he had been doing his military service his father had died, and all his property had been sold up. When he came back he was so appalled that he left to earn his living as a labourer, because he was a good workman, who, as he said, respected work, and had nothing but contempt for ordinary vagabonds, who he felt were good-for-nothings and layabouts. He liked Orschanow, sensing that he was sure of himself and had no malice, and was someone you could count on, who wouldn't land his companions in trouble, like so many would.

After a long silence, Perrin, who had been mulling things over, finally said, 'If you like, tomorrow we could set off together. It's always less tedious when there are two of you, and then again it'd be better for you, since you don't know this country. You could fall in with a bad lot who could cause you a lot of trouble. It's easily done.'

'Fine.'

Orschanow liked Perrin. And anyway, if he started to bore him, he only had to leave him. This provisional association with a vagabond, a labourer, appealed to him, as did everything which was thrown up by the randomness of the wandering life.

So they fell asleep, with no regrets and no worries: they were young and strong, and the road was there, welcoming anyone, leading off and away, it didn't matter where to. And the sun shone on everything, and man had bread to eat.

3

The sandy quayside pavements were awash with life. Goods of all kinds and colours piled up, flung together from the tops of dusty carts. There were stacks of pale, fresh wooden planks from the north, dotted with drops of pink resin, barrels of sulphur from Agde, etched with slim runnels of . greenish yellow, sacks of pale plaster, casks of wine stained with purple dregs, crates of powdered dyes leaking their pigments of deep indigo, emerald green, pale saffron, startling red lead.

Soft reflections glistened on the water under the setting sun, and golden lights sparkled in the vague eddies. The windows of the tall black houses around la Joliette harbour cast countless dreamy looks onto the lapping sea, where boats waited to dock or set off.

The dockers had finished loading the *Saint-Augustin*, bound for Oran, and were taking a break, stretching their strong arms. Their blue linen trousers were stained with tar and oil, their torsos seemed moulded into their blue and white vests, and loose red wool belts fell from their waists. Some of them wore sailors' berets, others old faded zouave or Spahi tarbooshes, cast-offs from Africa. The warm, rose-gold evening air brushed against their muscular necks and the bronzed contours of their faces, some worried and ill-defined, others pure and handsome.

Orschanow dressed like them now, and after barely a month he spoke their jargon, half Provençal, half maritime, spiced to a peppery Mediterranean flavour with exotic Arabic or Chinese words. Perrin had kept his fustian trousers and country hat, although he'd had to swap his smock for a vest, because of the men's teasing, which he took badly. He had come to this foreign land of the Midi, beside this sea which frightened him, reluctantly. He had been influenced by Orschanow and had followed him. Orschanow, though, was dazzled and intoxicated by the Mediterranean, after the smoky, gloomy northern ports and the steely inclemency of the northern sea. This was certainly the classic sea, the glistening sea, revelling in the glory of the sun, the deep purple sea-swell which had lapped against the sunny shores where human thought was first born. It was also the high road which led to all the dream-countries.

Orschanow had loved it and abandoned himself to it from the first opal morning when he had seen it from the white crests of the Nerthe Mountains. And then there was this maritime crowd, so noisy, so dazzling in its rags, so colourful in its display of misery, its pungent scents mingling together in the warm fermentation of its fertile soil!

*

Faced with Orschanow's eulogies, Perrin shrugged his shoulders. Obviously there were riches here, and work. You could find bread to eat, but you still had to beware of these types who would be all over you without knowing you and who would have the hide off your back if they could! Perrin had quickly seen through the surface *bon-homie* of the people of the Midi to the cunning, and brutal, uncontrolled passions beneath. He didn't like them, and couldn't see them as an artist would, as Orschanow did, and admire them as beautiful things in a beautiful light. He didn't know how to make an abstraction of their ugliness and moral decay. For him, they were lousy, shifty, knife-wielding rascals.

With his Slav suppleness, Orschanow knew how to adapt to any setting, could take on any colours, acquire any dialect, whilst remaining himself. The dockers liked him better than they liked Perrin, who was angular and reserved. They called Orschanow 'the Russian' and said he was a good sort.

*

Orschanow was sitting on the quayside, his bare feet swinging above the water, where bits of cork and scraps of red and yellow posters floated. He was dreaming. Near him a tall man from Piedmont with a pierced ear was trying to put on his belt, which kept dropping to the ground like a fiery snake. A small lop-sided lad called Henri with a malicious little goat's profile sang: '*Suona, suona la campana, Suona a matine suona!*' Since no one took up his refrain, he started to strut around. The others leant against a pile of sacks, smoking pipes, talking about the boats. The Arab Slimane half-lay on the ground tracing arabesques with his fingers in the hot dust of the flagstones. Working girls passed by, loose-haired, with red skirts and flowery aprons, like young ladies. Each of them carried her work folded in a scarf. They gave saucy looks to the dockers, who stood up, flexing their muscles. The girls pouted and began to giggle. A large black dog threw himself into the harbour and the men watched him swimming, his muzzle out of the water. All around him ever-widening circles of red-gold skimmed away until they hit the dark hulls of the boats. Orschanow let himself be carried along by the mood of the evening. In front of him he could see the jetty and the Mediterranean dockyards, their dull iron thud finished for the day, where the giant monsters of the maritime cargo-boats were forged, the far-off couriers to the Indies, China and the Oceanic islands. Beyond was Arenc and le Lazaret, and the slaughterhouses of le Mole where sombre silhouettes of Arabs in wild burnouses passed by, bringing in Algerian sheep. Further out, the rounded cove of l'Estaque, then the coast which sank into the wide mists of the sea. To the left, above Port-Vieux and the sailing-boats, above the forts of Saint-Jean and Entrecasteaux, Notre-Dame-de-la-Garde burned brilliantly in the red fire of the setting sun. A strong breath of life rose from Marseilles and its ports, an insistent call towards distant horizons, like a subtle and irresistible magic spell. For the first time, Orschanow realised that the universe did not end here on this quayside, that out there, beyond the soothing sea, were lands of sun and silence: Africa.

4

From behind the white peaks of the Nerthe Mountains, the sun rose red and rayless in a clear violet sky. On the quayside work was beginning again, as heavy carts clattered along, pulled by eight or ten huge square-rumped carthorses from Perche, with powerful necks and jangling collar-bells. Workers trudged towards their bondage, their espadrilles or bare feet padding softly on the dusty pavement. Stallholders went to and fro with large wicker baskets on their heads, singing in all keys in a lisping patois. A wave of red light flooded over the houses, boats, and quayside flagstones, breaking in a myriad of sparkles onto the ripples of the still harbour waters.

Orschanow and Perrin walked along in the splendour of the morning, carrying their bundles and following the lop-sided silhouette of little Henri, who clowned around in front of them. Perrin was pensive as usual, looking straight ahead, sucking his pipe. Once he had got over the shock of arriving in Marseilles he had quickly lost any curiosity for these maritime surroundings, becoming preoccupied with everyday matters and with work. A few days ago some new porters had undercut the wages on the boats and little Henri had taken advantage of the fact to persuade Orschanow and Perrin to go and look for work at la Fontaine des Tuiles, along by Estaque. It was much more fun, he reckoned. Above all, for him it was something different, something new. The lad couldn't live for more than two days in the same street, or even in the same area. He was a real Marseilles street-urchin, born to the scavenging and vaga-bond life.

Perrin had hesitated. This little monkey with his endless antics and his taste for thieving could land them all in trouble one day. Yet he followed Orschanow's lead again, accompanying him along the roads of Marseilles as he had done through France. The more Orschanow turned into a rough workman, the more Perrin respected the Russian's growing strength and capacity. You had to admit he managed pretty well nowadays. And then, Orschanow knew the trades they needed for these areas better than Perrin did.

*

Orschanow walked gaily, drinking in the beauty of things which, on that particular morning, were full of new har-monies of line and colour. Skirting the Lazaret quayside, they saw a mass of small-tonnage boats, odd, rusty little steam-boats with the incongruously sonorous names of old sailing-boats: *San Iréneo, Cartaghène, Santa Mater Dolorosa, Corinthe* . . . Their crews had left them for the spicy areas of the old town, and now they awaited the next departure, the next dream. For a moment Orschanow thought of becoming a sailor. Ever since the evening when he had sat daydreaming on the quay of la Joliette, watching the *Saint-Augustin* leave for Oran, he had been haunted by the idea of Africa, and above all of Muslim Africa. He thought of all his own atavistic links to Islam, through his maternal side, Tatar and nomadic. Just as he had on the morning he had left Geneva, Vera and his old life, Orschanow felt a wave of invigoration and life lifting him up and sweeping him on to conquer the world.

*

Little Henri hadn't lied: they did indeed find work, digging and carrying hot earth from the bottom of quarries which lay like open, bloody wounds in the green hills crowned with coastal pines. Under the baking sun they had toiled all day in the red dust amongst wild Sicilians and silent men from Piedmont. Between the two of them they could earn six francs a day: with that they could be happy. Little Henri, with his green squint eyes, grinned as they left for the day and suggested: 'What about going to eat some bread, cheese and sardines on the Estaque jetty? We could even pinch a couple of peaches from some woman's basket.'

'Blasted little thief!' Perrin cursed, indignant at the boy's villainy. As for Orschanow, he was indifferent to it. Little Henri was amusing, an artful little monkey. He was like a muddy weed growing out of the warm Mediterranean paving-stones. Wasn't that enough?

They went and sat down amongst the large black breakwaters of the jetty, which enclosed a silted, almost stagnant, bay full of brown seaweed and scuttling crabs. Perrin ate his bread and cheese slowly and carefully. It was the food of his part of the country. He didn't care much for sardines, convinced that they weren't nourishing. Orschanow ate very quickly as always, and now settled down on his elbow between two slippery breakwaters, facing the bay of Marseilles. In the distance Marseilles was bathed in rosy gold and dotted with the countless fiery reflections of windows and the pale glow of lighthouses and ships which were just lighting up. Over to the right there was the tall outline of the Bonne Mère Church on the ember-coloured chalk rock, then colours ranging from the rose madder of the Endoume cliffs, through the crimson of the arid rocks of Madrague de Montredon, to the deep violet of the sea, a swell of light which swamped the islands. On its own, far away, the pointed, dark rock of Maire Island burned in the middle of the fathomless waters. The great changing eye of the Planier lighthouse blinked out to the world. An immense sigh rose from the lulled waters.

Orschanow was engulfed by voluptuous drowsiness. As if in a dream, without emotion or haste, he thought it would be good to set off for unknown lands across the sea on such an evening of calm obliteration, with sweet melancholy in his heart, without bitterness, and with a definitive renouncement of all his past, of all that he had ever been, and with the sure intuition that he would never return.

5

Eleven o'clock on a summer morning on the quayside streets. The rattling of heavy carts, the endless rumblings of the maritime town, had stopped for a moment in the exhaustion of midday. In the harbour the muddy violet water lay immobile and heavy, as if thickened by the heat, with oily, metallic slicks oscillating gently on its surface.

Under red- and grey-striped canvas tents in the middle of the square stalls were being filled with colourful, strong-smelling food: raw tomatoes, green peppers, black olives, red chilis, fat mauve and white onions, shrivelled salamis, fried golden-brown fish with transparent slices of lemon, whole greenish lemons amongst black mussel-shells, heavy muscat grapes the colour of pale honey, light, white loaves, blackish-red cherries. It was a treat for the eyes, alongside little stoves improvised from collapsed old petrol cans on which peppery Marseilles dishes cooked, yellow with saffron. The smell of oil rose from these stalls and clouds of flies buzzed around. Half-naked dockers exhausted with fatigue and heat left the quays and came along in groups. First they stopped at the fountain and, one after the other, washed their hands and shook them dry. Then they crowded in a compact mass in front of the stalls, exchanging coarse jokes in patois, and bartering and arguing to the accompaniment of the jangle of copper coins. And from all this hungry crowd rose the strong savage smell of male sweat. Orschanow would dig into the oily and peppery food with its onions and olives. Perrin shrugged his shoulders, preferring a good litre of white wine, a *baguette* and a little cheese – less heavy on the stomach, he felt.

Holding greasy papers flat in one hand, their bread under their arms and their drink in the other hand, the workmen ran to find places in the shade of the houses along the quayside. They ate avidly off their knees, sitting on the edge of the pavement, their feet in the dry gutter full of straw and rubbish. Every moment an arm would lift a bottle of red or white wine, a head would tilt back, brown neck muscles would ripple.

Orschanow always finished eating before the others, and now he stretched out on the pavement, his beret over his eyes, not to sleep, but to dream.

*

He was calm, tired, and free of any desires. Thinking of his new life, he was amazed that, after the sufferings and doubts of the last few years, it had been so simple and easy to make himself happy, in the only way, given his nature, that he could be.

It was enough for him to isolate himself, to come down to the simple and rough areas of town where he felt at ease and was accepted by everyone because he seemed to talk and act like them, although in reality he stayed the loner that he always had been and always would be. Unlike most intellectuals, Dmitri wasn't bothered by poor people and simpletons, because they never penetrated his private world of feelings and ideas. To be free, you had to be alone, always, everywhere, and above all amongst people. Orschanow felt sorry for men's miserable need to band together in moral collectives, to offer themselves to the yoke of other people's insufferable tyranny and crushing judgement. Wandering and alone in a world in which he could always stay unknown, Orschanow was really free. He thought and acted as he wanted to, and no one could pretend to control his thoughts, since all he needed to do was to leave, at the first clash of views, and set off on the road again.

Stretched out on the paving-stones, his hardened limbs weary, Orschanow felt his chest expand with joy and pride at the thought of his complete emancipation. Then he suddenly thought of Vera, and his heart jumped a little. It always gave him a delicious feeling to think of her, to tell himself, not cruelly but wistfully, that he would never see her again, that he wouldn't even know anything about her, because he wouldn't write to her, wouldn't keep any link between him and his past.

With his eyes closed, Dmitri again saw Vera, the lover he had so long and so ardently desired, with whom he had lived out his most erotic fantasies. Vera's short, silky black curls, her enigmatic smile, the undulating line of her virginal body, going from the shoulder to the knee in fluid curves. At the memory of it Orschanow was tormented with regrets. He stretched out and opened his eyes to see the sun dancing on the ships and the harbour water. Then he calmed down again and smiled: at life, at love, at the way things changed.

*

As evening fell, with some traces of his midday reverie still burning within him, Orschanow left his comrades and climbed slowly towards the seedy areas where the brutal life of the hot city already throbbed in streets filled with bareheaded, painted girls in short skirts, who smoked as they waited for the men, the sailors, dockers, soldiers, the *nervi*. He strolled along unhurriedly in the hot night filled with the smell of musk and women, now and then going into bars and sitting down without drinking. He no longer drank much, since leaving Russia.

These old streets full of prostitution, misery and crime, full of songs and drunkenness, were in tune with his mood. Instead of disgust or curiosity, Orschanow felt at one with all the blind desire surging through this part of town. Finally, going back down towards the port through humid backstreets, he saw a woman in a red smock with a canary-yellow scarf tied over extraordinary black hair falling half-loose over her shoulders. She was very young, and her pale, almost bloodless face had a strange Mediterranean beauty, indefinably mixed and complex.

'*Digo, pitchoun!*' A fat woman with a flowing dress and flowers in her blonde hair was calling Orschanow. The dark-haired girl, leaning against a wall, said nothing. She didn't even smile. Orschanow noticed she was barefoot. He went up to her.

'Where's your room?'

'*Vengo.*'

And, unhurriedly, with deep indifference, she led the way through a dark, smelly corridor. In the room there was a bed, a white wood table, two broken wicker stools, a cupboard. Damp black stains on the low ceiling and the peeling wallpaper made the room even darker. The woman unbolted the door, then began to undress, still without a word. And this woman's silence, which suited her strange beauty, finally seduced Orschanow's senses. Like her abrupt gestures and her throaty, almost rasping voice, this girl's love-making was bitter and brutal, without the sentimentality or spinelessness of most girls.

*

Orschanow woke up. The blinds were still half-open and the blueish light of morning slid over to the bed where the girl slept, her head sunk in the pillow. He could only see her vague outline under the coarse sheet, and the heavy mass of her hair. He turned towards the window. Somewhere a caged canary began to sing. A breath of fresh air ruffled the curtains, blowing like a caress onto Orschanow's chest in the open neck of his workman's shirt. A sudden feeling of tenderness came over him. His soul felt pure and new. He was happy to be alive, happy to know that outside day was breaking and the wind was freshening on the sea, happy to think that he was going to toil under the sun with comrades whom he liked. Yet at the same time he was happy to know that in a few days, inevitably, he would leave these people and these places and go elsewhere, far away, beyond the Mediterranean, and drink deeply from other sources of pleasure and sorrow.

6

Towards the end of August anger began to gather around the quays like a storm. Every day Italian boats would deposit poverty-stricken labourers on the quayside, all skin and bone, their faces angular and clean-shaven, their backs bent under meagre bundles. As soon as they arrived, they would slink off to the seedy parts of town. The next day they would come back to the harbour and accost the foremen, cap in hand, humbly offering their knotty paupers' arms for a pittance. And the wages got lower and lower. Whenever a workman protested he was sacked, since there was an inexhaustible supply of Italians.

One morning a brawl broke out in front of the transatlantic landing-stage as some new Calabrians turned up looking for work. The dockers pushed them to one side, hurling threats and insults at them. The two groups came to blows. Knives flashed, and blood flowed. Ten workmen were sacked that afternoon, but they stayed on the quayside until nightfall in an angry, threatening bunch. In the dockyard, an unidentified docker knocked out an Italian with his bare fists and then drowned him.

Orschanow's fellow labourers began to tell him it was up to him to take charge and lead them, since he was the most educated of them all. They had a right to defend themselves, but only he could talk to the bosses and authorities in language they understood. At first he resisted: he was only a docker like the rest of them and didn't want to be a leader. Not that he wasn't affected just like the others by the cut in wages, and by the bullying of the increasingly arrogant and argumentative foremen, it was just that it didn't matter to him. It was only the fluke of his vagabond life which had brought him here. He felt at a distance from these people and didn't want to set himself up as their leader, which would do no good to anyone. He knew that with a minimal effort he could dominate them all and make them putty in his hands, but he wanted to stay a dreamer, and solitary.

But when the situation deteriorated and the initially peaceful meetings turned nasty, he found himself caught up in the fray. He enjoyed the sudden excitement, and no longer had the courage to be self-effacing. He found himself inevitably becoming the leader of his group of companions, partly to save himself from their lack of understanding and the appallingly incoherent disarray of their excitable minds. High-flown phrases and talk of revenge would inflame them, and they would mix up verses from the 'Internationale' with childish and ferocious chauvinistic gibes. Massacre the *Macaronis*, the *Babi*, who were taking away the livelihood of the French! They themselves were the flotsam and jetsam of all races, Latin and others, whom the Mediterranean's ebb had landed on the coast. But all of them, even

95

Slimane the Arab, even Juaneto from Mahon, claimed sudden allegiance to France.

Alcohol flowed, fuelling their anger, increasing their tension, fogging their already feeble judgement. In spite of the fact that he could clearly see their weaknesses and the pointlessness of their struggle, Orschanow supported them, finding their anger pitiful but admirable. And, after all, hadn't he wasted precious days long ago in revolutionary meetings, in pointless waffling discussions? Whilst here the same ideas, however confused, had suddenly been brought into the tragic arena of real life. Why should he avoid them now?

At the first mention of the word 'strike', strangers appeared talking of solidarity, of organisation, of class warfare. Here were the ideas which had fired Orschanow in the past, which had been his credo, which he had fought for, being repeated with less bitterness and less fantasy. The men mixed with the labourers, and tried to organise them. But they came from factions which didn't agree amongst themselves, and so they dragged the dockers into their quarrels. What astonished Orschanow and made him indignant was that the confusion which reigned amongst the workers didn't worry the popular orators in the least. Quite the opposite: some of them managed to turn it to their advantage.

No one thought of helping the workers to understand their situation better. They treated them like a servile flock to be herded onwards to the conquest of capital. The workers were to them an amorphous and confused force, but one which could be manipulated, if you knew how, to sweep away the ruins of the old society. There was no attempt to inculcate any kind of conscious will in them; brute matter was all that was needed, to be subjugated and transformed into an instrument, not to be shaped. Orschanow could see that these men didn't really like the workers, and even despised them. He had already met dogmatists of this kind in Russia, but not many, since the rest of the revolutionaries hadn't taken to them. Their ruthlessness didn't appeal to the Russians' natural idealism and compassion.

In a meeting one evening Orschanow heard such a speaker trying to get the men to join a group which he knew had been started at one of the great northern trading ports, and was nearly driven to speak up against him. But he bit his tongue, and by the time he left his anger had subsided, and he found himself smiling, knowing that he alone of the ten or twelve intellectuals present genuinely loved the men, in all their misery and weakness. He loved them just as they were, without reproaching them or despising them. But as he returned in the warm, quiet night to the barge where he was sleeping he felt a sudden sadness. The strike was going to happen. There would be awful hardship. Blood would be shed, energies would be wasted for nothing at all, whole lives would be the poorer for it. However it was conducted, whether skilfully or dogmatically, the strike would come to nothing. At this point Orschanow fantasised longingly about hordes of these long-suffering people raging through Marseilles, through the whole world, on an apocalyptic journey of destruction. But he wouldn't be the one to tell them the truth, nor to lead them. He would just continue to collect their sorrow drop by drop in his heart, as if in a chalice.

Yet, within his group, Orschanow spoke up once or twice. He tried to warn the workers off any tack which was not strictly related to the question of their wages. He advised them to put some money aside now, while they

were still earning something. Above all he warned them
not to get involved in any political party, and to stay
workmen, simply demanding their right to a hard-earned
living. The dockers agreed with him as he spoke, since his
point of view was so simple and sensible, and since he
worked alongside them and had often given them good
advice before. But then the strike-promoters returned,
bought drinks for them all and fanned their imaginations
with grandiose words. So once more they ran through
the harbour cheering and shouting, drunk on alcohol and
raucous noise.

Orschanow had his moments of revolt and exasperation.
He sometimes found himself detesting these stupid men
who only obeyed people who despised them and didn't give
a damn for them. One day, in a meeting where some
spokesman was talking of them getting their own back on
the bourgeois – interrupted at every minute by cries of
'Death to all exploiters!' – Orschanow said, 'If the workers
do manage to get rid of the bourgeois, it'll be you lot who
will have to be swept away the next day, because you would
simply have taken their place.'

The speaker tried to stir up the workers against their comrade, who stood calmly in front of them. But one of Orschanow's mates, a stubborn, taciturn old sailor, took his pipe
out from between yellowing teeth and said, 'We don't give a
damn. When it comes to it, we shan't let up. If we kill a
bourgeois, everyone will be in for it. Blood goes to the head
even more than drink does. I saw that in Indo-China: once
we started on a village, we annihilated it.'

'You're right,' cried another young man, 'when we've
got rid of those who are exploiting us now, we'll have
plenty of energy left to take on those who try to replace
them. You'll see.'

98

The speaker was taken aback, much to Orschanow's satisfaction. He shrugged his shoulders and left. If he had kept on on that tack, he would have found himself taking on the despicable role of rabble-rouser.

7

At last a day came when the ports were deserted. Around the barges and the crates of merchandise stacked on the quayside, only customs officials in red and blue wandered distractedly. Not a single docker had turned up. The strike had been declared the previous evening, word running through the meetings and the cafés like wildfire. Late into the night the men had been singing songs of freedom and shouting, 'Long live the strike!' Orschanow had walked through their exultation with other members of his group. The boy Henri expressed their joy in his own terms: 'What luck! Tomorrow, instead of flogging ourselves to death on the boats, we can go to Madrague or Estaque and fish for a *bouillabaisse*!' Naively, the dockers rejoiced in these first days of unemployment. They still had a penny or two, they could eat, and they wouldn't have to work. Then, when the bosses had had enough, they would give in and the Italians, the despised *Babi*, would be sent packing back to their wretched country with a good kick up the arse.

It was so obvious, so easy! Orschanow looked at them on the first evening of the strike. They were happy and elated, their eternal Latin chatter punctuated by bursts of laughter. Why point out to them that they were wrong to rejoice, that soon they would be dying of hunger and that, even if they succeeded in getting rid of the Italians, this little victory would cost them endless hardship and rancour? After all, he told himself, they were snatching a few hours of happier, more intense life from the hard monotony of their servitude.

The next morning, as the others went up to the old town to celebrate, Orschanow left on his own for the pine forests of Estaque, where he lay down on the hot earth and day-dreamed, surrounded by the good scent of pine resin. He would wait – out of pride and curiosity – until the strike had ended, and then he would set off into the blue again, no matter where. He would go alone, without Perrin, since he had begun to weary of his companion's common sense and down-to-earth principles. Perrin had kept quiet throughout the meetings preceding the strike. But when the men had decided they would stop work, he told Orschanow in his usual plain fashion, 'If that's the way it is, then we won't work either. It would be piggish to work when your mates have a grievance – even though to me their politics are a pain in the neck. As for these gasbags in the cafés, well, I say they're all good for nothings, just taking the rest of us for a ride. And what about all these *mocos* who blather on all the time, they're empty vessels making too much noise, that's my view.' But Perrin stayed imper-turbable and uninvolved, like the good workman that he was, and just waited patiently.

Orschanow had decided that he wanted to take to the road alone this time, with just his dreams, and that meant an amicable parting with Perrin. He was grateful for his early help, but once again he was going to quit a friendship he had got used to, just as he had left his previous friends, his student life and Vera herself. Exile and separation held a great, melancholy charm for him. Above all he loved the moment of setting off, when he was alone again with his memories and the ghosts of his recent past.

*

Orschanow foresaw great troubles as a result of the strike. There would certainly be fights between the strikers and the Italians. The *Babi* were still working, more in some docks than others. In the first flush of the strike, no one went to harass them. The men just talked about them contemptuously. But it wouldn't always be like that. When alcohol had gone to some people's heads, there were bound to be disturbances. If they went and tried to stop the Italians working, Orschanow would go along too – after all, wasn't it logical and necessary? He had no hatred for these sober worker-ants who had come from far away to sell their hard-worked bodies for a pittance. He felt as sorry for them as he did for the others. But it would be war, inevitably it would be war.

Orschanow wondered whether the crowd's rage or fear would have any effect on him, the solitary individualist so jealous of his liberty. He thought not. In any case, he knew that in a few days he would have the opportunity to find out.

8

It was a hot, moonless evening, and groups of dockers were crowding through the back streets behind the harbour, singing revolutionary songs and waving the red flag. They forged ahead as if marching to conquer the town. Sometimes they would stop and let out a yell of 'Death to the *Babi*! Death to them!' and then station themselves menacingly in front of the Italian bars and cafés, which closed one by one as they approached. They marched around like this for some time, content to shout, for the most part without being tempted to go into the cafés. But the heat grew overwhelming, and their shouting and singing made them thirsty. Then drink began to flow, rousing their excitable Latin blood. Waves of anger rippled through the confused groups and ruffled the red folds of the flags they were holding at arms' length. The songs would be interrupted by more cries of 'Death to the *Babi*!' which echoed from one end of the port to the other, in the salty air of the idle docks.

The police arrived and charged into groups of strikers to disperse them. Orschanow was still following his group; neither he nor Perrin had drunk anything. Perrin was quite calm: why get into a stew? If you didn't want the *Macaronis* to work, you had to go to the dockyards where they were working, in the morning, and not run like idiots from café to café. 'If it weren't letting workmates down, I'd be off,' he said, irritated by all this commotion, which his common sense told him was pointless.

But Orschanow was mesmerised by the savage beauty of the crowd, by these healthy, robust men in their working clothes – some in striped sailors' vests, some in red vests, some in black waistcoats – suddenly dignified by their anger, their broad shoulders highlighted by the pools of alternating red and blue from the gas and electric lights. This annihilation of individuality into one body, into one delirious force, was a curious spectacle for him, as someone who understood what was going on. But soon a kind of troubled frenzy began to take hold of him, too. This, he told himself irrationally, was the real revolution: not the sermonising, but this, the real thing, out on the wretched streets of a city of misery and unfair labour, borne along by a wave of men weary of hardship.

Suddenly the group in front of Orschanow's came to a halt. Heads jostled, cries broke out: the dockers had come up against the police. 'Death, death to the *Babi*!' The policemen's voices commanding them to break up were drowned by the workers' clamour. There was a scuffle, and the police drew their swords, which flashed here and there in the dark confusion of the crowd. Then suddenly they heard rhythmic footsteps, the dull thud of advancing troops: 'Soldiers! Soldiers!' 'The bastards'll have our guts,' Perrin grumbled, but Orschanow wasn't listening: it had all gone to his head, and he was pushing forward unconsciously, as if inebriated. Now they were surely going to fight, and instead of regretting all this, as he had done a few days before, he suddenly accepted the inevitability of a clash and a struggle. They were unarmed, and would be fighting with their fists, with their feet. Orschanow pushed through to the front of the crowd, where the men were hurling abuse at the police and pushing them back towards the soldiers waiting motionless a few steps away, their weapons by their feet.

'Pigs,' cried a workman, 'you come from the people,

perhaps you're even from Marseilles, aren't you ashamed to come and hit out at your brothers?' The soldiers didn't flinch. As the workers continued to drive them back, the officer gave a curt command, and the police charged. The mêlée barely lasted a few minutes. Orschanow, blinded, tossed about in the formidable crush of bodies, hit out indiscriminately. One of the officers' swords brushed against him, and instinctively he reached out, twisted the man's arm and grabbed his sword. Then there was a gasp and a groan, and the man fell under the stampede of the crowd. Orschanow awoke from his mesmerised state. He had killed a man – possibly even the chief of police. He had to get out.

The workers began to give way under the pressure of police and soldiers, realising they were going to be surrounded and arrested. Orschanow found the scene stupid and sinister. He slipped away through the crowd, and finally reached the quayside, alone, walking slowly along the Fraternité quay, and along by the Rive-Neuve, where everything was deserted and calm. Then he quickened his step, almost running around the hill. That was it for this evening. They wouldn't find him before daybreak. Tomorrow he would think what to do. He would leave Marseilles, and get back on the open road. He thought of Perrin with a pang of pity. His poor friend must have been arrested, because he certainly wouldn't have managed to get away. What would become of him?

Orschanow found some waste land and fell asleep thinking that no one could do anything about all this and everyone had to fulfil his own destiny. As for him, he would carry on alone, as he had always wanted to.

9

Orschanow sat at a table with Perrin in the darkest corner of a bar on the Rive-Neuve which was meant to look like a grotto, with cemented rocks and shells and red lighting. He was working out what to do. In their stories of the previous evening's fracas the morning papers mentioned that a police inspector had been killed by a docker who was known as 'the Russian'. That was quite enough for him to be found. Orschanow read and re-read the line, then lifted his head suddenly as a man walked in and came up to them. It was Lombard, one of their group.

'Well, old mate, we're in a right mess and no doubt about it. That was a dirty piece of work last night! On the other hand, I don't give a damn, I've got my own plan worked out. I've just come in for a drink and then I'm off.'

'Off where?'

'Nowhere special. I'm off to the Foreign Legion, that's all. It seems to me there's some fun to be had in Africa! And plenty of bread around.'

'Now that's an idea!' Perrin exclaimed.

A silence fell between them. Sitting out on the pavement a young fishwife was shouting hoarsely and provocatively in front of her basket of wares: 'Mussels, wallflowers, beautiful wallflowers – come and get them!'

Lombard was explaining his plan.

'It's a great idea – you don't even need any papers to get there!'

Africa! Orschanow listened raptly to his comrade.

'You know, Lombard,' he said at last, 'I think I'm going to do the same as you.'

'It's the best thing you can do, given you're up to your eyes in trouble, like me. I seem to remember socking two coppers last night because they were trying to nick me. I bashed their heads against each other, smash! and they collapsed on the pavement. And then of course people came and walked all over them.'

'Another glass, and then we'll go. Are you coming, Perrin?'

'I'm certainly not going to be left behind. Africa's a long way from home, but I wouldn't be alone if you were there.'

Still he didn't make a move, wanting to discuss a little more before he decided.

'What about your freedom, what do you think about that?'

Lombard was quick to reply: 'We'd take it with us.'

'And then, I'm a foreigner . . .'

'Just say you're Swiss, you idiot!'

Perrin was reluctantly convinced. He briskly ordered a round of drinks: 'We must wash it all down!'

Orschanow knew quite well that he was about to sacrifice five years of his life. But at least he would be on that African soil which had attracted his imagination for so long – that was enough.

As they left they all bought sprigs of flowers from a ragged slip of a girl and stuck them in their hats and buttonholes. Then, a little muzzy from their aperitifs, they linked arms and walked off triumphally, blocking the pavement. But a delivery of planks halted their glorious progress, so they took a short-cut up towards Pierre-Puget Promenade. Perrin sang in his tone-deaf voice: 'I'm off to join the Legion, All for the love of a blonde,' and dribbled onto his peasant's moustache.

10

Orschanow and Perrin followed Lombard to the recruiting office, where they completed the brief formalities. Orschanow called himself Kasimirsky, a Pole who had returned from Brazil, where he had tried to settle. Perrin called himself Swiss, which he was, and Lombard volunteered to be Belgian. When they asked them which of the two regiments they wanted to be sent to, someone who seemed to know what he was talking about nudged Orschanow and said: 'Say you want to go into the Second Battalion, it's easier there.'

Now they were at the Saint-Jean Fortress, that old outpost of the Legion, waiting with a dozen others for the boat to leave for Oran. Orschanow realised the extent of what he had done: he had signed on for five years, he had given up his freedom, he was now just a pawn without a will of his own. And yet he felt no despair about it, only the same mixture of sadness and happiness he had felt when he left Geneva. He also sensed that, paradoxically, he would be more free under his legionnaire's greatcoat than he had been in his student's clothes. Among the men who were going to be his companions he would be able to keep himself to himself, to be unknown, therefore free.

And so it was without any qualms that he looked out onto Marseilles, although it was now so familiar to him, and although he had become fond of it. One last time he walked along la Joliette where he had encountered the thrill of sun and warm air for the first time in his life, where he had had the unforgettable revelation of Mediterranean life. Now he was off to Africa, new and unknown to him, whose magnetic appeal had captivated him one day and never left him.

The volunteers, in an assortment of clothes, came out into the courtyard of the fortress accompanied by uniformed corporals and a sergeant. With them were two emaciated and terrified youngsters who were being sent off to the African battalions, and soldiers in dusty uniforms who were being confined to barracks.

Orschanow followed the detachment, feeling full of energy, and glad to be out of the prison-like fortress. The *Berry*, a ship belonging to the Transports Maritimes would depart when it had loaded its cargo. How the quayside had changed! There was heavy silence all around, and soldiers were patrolling up and down, amongst the last load of cargo lying abandoned in the sun.

They lined up the soldiers and the new recruits on the *Berry*'s foredeck and the sergeant read the rollcall. Then they were left to chat and smoke. They had been numbered, rounded up, loaded on board. They were now the captain's responsibility, cargo to be unloaded at Oran.

How often and how enviously Orschanow had watched these boats slowly weigh anchor and leave for Africa! Now he was happy, his wish was fulfilled. And yet he was no longer the free vagabond, master of his fate, but only a soldier, and it was a thought he suddenly found sobering. Next to him, two recruits were talking, and one of them, a very young, pale, still beardless lad, seemed to be bitterly regretting his decision. The other, a tall, fair-haired young man, well-dressed and with a fine, northern profile, shrugged his shoulders. 'Come on, Bernaert, don't worry about it, the sun won't forget to shine on you tomorrow!' The stranger was right. The sun would rise tomorrow, and it would be a hotter, fierier sun in a deeper blue sky.

The Mediterranean would lap with bluer waves and new horizons would open up to the exile's eager eyes.

Orschanow shook himself as if after a bad dream, and leant against the railings, watching Marseilles gradually recede into the distance. He wondered if he would ever see it again, and sensed that he would not. Why return, why try to start again?

After supper, the passengers settled down for the night. The soldiers were given blankets, and some of them gave theirs to three working women who were nursing babies. With the unspoken camaraderie of poor people, they helped the civilians prepare their bunks. Orschanow had given up his blanket. He stretched out on the hatchway to the hold and, his arms crossed beneath his head, stared as the clear night fell on the violet sea. In the distance the Planier lighthouse blinked on, and above him the stars began to light up in the watery sky. The *Berry* rocked gently, as if balancing on the swell from deep below. Orschanow looked at the rigging, watching the beams from the ship's two beacons slowly flash round and round in front of the constellations. And he felt all his regrets and fears melting away, as if he were infused with the immense calm of the night and the sea. Tears of contentment started to his eyes. Oh, the feeling of renouncing everything, of being poor, of going through the world without family, without a home and without friends ... Nothing should be regretted or expected, you should just let yourself be carried along by the waves of life, as the indolent *Berry* was being carried along by the soft wash of the benevolent Mediterranean.

11

The *Berry*'s hull slipped softly, almost languorously, through the sea. On the bow deck the homeless poor in search of a more clement land, one without hunger and harsh winters, slept with their faces to the sky, oblivious to everything. The ship hit a current and rocked, and Orschanow woke with a start to find himself lying on rough canvas now drenched with salt water. To the right a lighthouse flashed on the horizon, next to another with a steady red beam. It was the Balearics.

Orschanow lit a cigarette and felt a delicious airy sense of well-being. At some moments since leaving Marseilles he had been impatient to arrive at the longed-for Barbary coast; at others, like now, in the silence and solitude of the night, he wanted the voyage to go on forever. He was happy.

Since the troubles at the docks had started, and he had become mixed up again in the agitation of men's affairs, he had not felt this infinitely sweet sensation of calm melancholy and peace of mind which he called happiness, the only happiness, as he knew very well, accessible to his nature. And now that it was all over and he was back on his own, embarking on a new phase of his existence, he felt overjoyed to recognise this feeling again. What did tomorrow matter, or these five years of servitude? Under the harsh yoke he would remain the most fortunate and proudest of men, because he carried his happiness inside him. In the eyes of the world, he would appear a wretched failure, doomed to the most miserable of existences. Yet in all conscience he considered himself the happiest man alive.

He watched the lights of the Balearics gradually merge into the great stellar glow spread over the sea, and fell back into sleep, rocked by the *Berry*'s monotonous movement.

12

The ship was manoeuvring alongside the dock, to the accompaniment of the excited bustle of arrival. There was a strange, indefinable and pungent scent in the air, which came over in warm gusts. They could see high, arid hills, an old Moorish citadel, red cliffs, all bathed in a hot, golden light. A feeling of dreamy, languid sensuality hung in the air.

The soldiers and recruits followed a corporal who called them one by one according to his list. Then the detachment started the climb up the hot slopes running alongside dusty gardens full of screeching cicadas. Orschanow followed his noisy companions in silence, feasting his eyes on the alternate light and deeply-coloured shade, and the florid, gaudy colours in the fierce bustle of the Moorish populace. For him, it seemed, who had fallen for the country without knowing it, the African soil had decked itself out superbly and royally.

*

The small train went along slowly, as if it were going for a stroll, passing tiny stations, pale golden fields, vineyards ringing with the song of Moroccan gatherers, russet hills flecked with olive trees. The narrow wooden compartments were full of laughing and singing soldiers. Less boisterous, more eager perhaps for the next stage, the recruits had herded together, many of them young men from Alsace or Germany who had deserted or absconded and were exchanging military service under their own skies for another, far away. Lombard, the 'Belgian', had bought some papers and was reading, while the tall young blonde man was looking at the countryside absentmindedly. With an almost disdainful reserve, he kept the others at a distance, except the 'Belgian', with whom he occasionally exchanged short, ironic remarks, in an indefinable accent.

A man from Alsace asked Orschanow where he came from, and, forgetting what he had said to the Legion, Orschanow told him he was Russian. The tall, taciturn young man turned towards him and gave him a long, hard stare. Orschanow guessed he was a compatriot, but they didn't exchange another word. As far as Orschanow was concerned, he was completely caught up in the new adventure in this unknown Africa, and felt no urge to talk to others at all.

The calm, comfortable landscape of the Algerian colonists passed by in the blue light of morning – Perrégaux, a little Spanish village covered with luxurious vegetation, with shady, cool avenues of eucalyptus and peppers. At the top of the hill was a large dammed *wadi* forming a small, clear lake at the foot of hills wooded with pine and sweet-scented thuyas. Further on was the plain, field upon field, immense vines with leaves reddened by the sun.

Suddenly, after the village of Thiersville, everything changed. No more vineyards, no more farms. Just the infinite, wild, naked steppe, speckled with countless dwarf palm trees, and with the occasional white patch of a flock of sheep, guarded by small Arab shepherds who would run down with excited cries to see the train pass by. How this bitter and burnt steppe resembled the one near Petchal, where Orschanow had learnt to dream, and where he had fallen in love with the wandering life!

On the horizon a heat-haze blurred the distant mountains and the plain seemed to stretch on endlessly, right up to the sky. The African steppe, hot and sterile, the property of eternity, and jealously ruled by the only light which existed there, was a revelation to Orschanow, initiating him instantly into its magic power. Now he scorned the pleasant, Italianate landscape of the Tell, and fell for these magnificent, serene steppes, in spite of the vaguely menacing mystery which hovered over their distant fiery horizons.

At Nazereg, there were hills full of thuyas and juniper trees, and the track passed through bushes thick with bird-song and the screech of cicadas. Then, towards the end of the day came Saïda, sad Saïda, set in rock and stone.

As the recruits leant out of the windows, curious to see their place of exile, the fair-haired young man said, with his ironic smile, 'Well now, this is where all azure dreams end up . . . here's the refuge you come back to, fatally, in spite of everything, when you've been here once. What the hell? You can live here.'

Orschanow looked out at Saïda. Everything was reddish at this time of year: the earth, the arid hills crowned with jagged rocks, the ramparts, the tiled roofs of the houses, the roads.

PART THREE

I

The new recruits to the Twenty-second Company of the Second Battalion were lining up on the parched ground. To the east were the Legion's quarters, the long, blank walls and tiled roofs of the barracks, and the blackish skeletons of trees in the courtyard.

As they had neared Saïda, the weather had suddenly freshened, and a wind had begun to sweep the valley. The recruits were back in winter, a strange winter which was like autumn in their home country. The mountains were covered in snow, making an odd contrast with the persistent greenery of the enormous, knotty olive trees and the spindly eucalyptus.

When they arrived, the 'blues', as they were called because of their blue uniforms, had been hustled from office to office and had finally been more or less kitted out. Perrin was not as much of a sight as the rest, since, having been a soldier before, he swiftly returned to his old habits and knew how to rig himself out in a regimental way. But Orschanow felt thoroughly uncomfortable in his red trousers, which were all new and stiff; his long jacket flapped against his legs; it all seemed to him like a disguise. When they looked at each other, he and Perrin burst out into childlike laughter.

'You'll have to get used to it, you feel really queer the first few days. But you adapt. I know the ropes a bit, I'll teach you how.'

Perrin was rediscovering his memories of three years of military service, and found some satisfaction in it all. What annoyed him was to sleep in a tent in weather which had turned quite bitter. Towards evening, the mountain wind would furiously shake the poor little Bedouin tents.

*

At five o'clock, after soup, the 'blues' were dazed with exhaustion, even though they had done no work. They would be presented to the colonel the next day, and then their training would begin.

'I've a feeling that it's best to get into the trainee corporal section,' Perrin said. 'It's tougher, but at least you end up in a better position.'

'Ah, but is the daily workload more?'

'That it certainly is.'

'Well in that case it's not for me. Let's rest first and take time to get to know the people we're going to be living with. We'll always have time afterwards.'

Sitting in front of their tent, Orschanow and Perrin looked at the camp, almost deserted at this time, the one, long-awaited moment of freedom in the whole day. Orschanow felt that these would be his hours of freedom for the next five years. From five until nine he could wander at will in the town and the countryside, free to think and dream. If some day he began to find the soldier's life almost impossible, he would always have as a consolation these four daily hours which were his alone, and which no one could take away.

A tall, fair soldier, with steely, intelligent eyes, came up to them and asked for a light. He lit his long German pipe and sat down in front of Orschanow and Perrin.

'Where d'you two come from?'

'I'm Swiss and my pal is Russian. What about you?'

'I'm Bulgarian. I'm part of your section, that's why I ask.'

Then he spoke directly to Orschanow in Russian, with a strong accent. 'You see, I used to be a student. I studied law at Kiev. Then I got caught up in the troubles. I got away, and after all kinds of episodes, ended up here. Life is tough here because of the brutes all around us. There's no solidarity amongst legionnaires; it's every man for himself and the devil take the hindmost.'

'But you can have an inner life, all the same.'

'If only there were something to read, some way of exchanging ideas. But without books or intellectual society, how can you live?'

'Listen, my friend, I gave up student life voluntarily, to become a labourer and a vagabond. It was circumstances and' – he hesitated – 'also a passion to come to Africa which made me join up. Well, for two years I've been absolutely free and I haven't opened a book, I haven't even had the urge to read a newspaper.'

'I don't understand you.'

'What's the point of reading? What's the point of even thinking about it? There are other pleasures, better and more intense pleasures.'

'What are they then? What could be better than calm intellectual enjoyment, and improving yourself, to be ready for the fight which is incumbent on all of us intellectuals?'

'Fight? A fight for what? It seems like bourgeois egoism to say: make out as best you can. But it isn't, it's the only advice a real libertarian can give. By what right do you trespass on the liberty of others?'

'You have to wake people up to the truth.'

'Someone who's asleep isn't suffering. And even if he's dreaming, he's suffering less than someone who's awake.

No, you have to look to other resources, to look for life everywhere, in pleasure and in suffering, because it's in both.'

'And what about you, where have you found it?'

'I was a medical student. I was engaged to an intelligent and beautiful woman, but one morning I left it all, with my worldly goods on my shoulder, to work on the land and to enjoy life, with this peasant here. Oh, how happy we've been for two years out on the road, in the fields, as dockers in Marseilles!'

'How passionate you are about it!' the Bulgarian said without irony, but with a sad smile. 'I can easily recognise your Russian blood, impassioned and morbid at the same time, which runs hot and highly-charged and burns your heart. I'm a Slav, too, but quite different: you're men for sensations, and me, I'm a man for ideas.'

'It's not true,' Orschanow said brusquely.

'What do you mean, it's not true?'

'No, it can't be true, because if you were only a man of ideas, if Slav blood didn't flow through your veins, you wouldn't be here.'

The Bulgarian blanched a little and stared at him. 'It's true, of course, what you say.'

Orschanow wondered why he, who was usually so quiet with people he didn't know, had opened his heart to this stranger, who had all the tendencies and ideas that he himself had fled two years ago. When he thought about it, he smiled: what a childish thing! It was just the fact of having heard, for the first time since he left, the music of the Russian tongue, which had overwhelmed him with emotion and touched him to the quick.

He got up and went off on his own to calm down. A sudden metaphor came to him: he was in a new mine, forced to exploit it for five years. The riches which he could extract would be his. So he must take them all, thoroughly exhausting the mine. For him, there were no mines without hidden treasure. To extract it would be hard labour, but he mustn't give up.

He shook himself and his courage returned. How stupid and blind men were! All of them, consciously or not, were frantically chasing after happiness, yet it eluded most of them, when all the time it was right there for the taking. All of them were the slaves of people and things, to which they held on, or by which they let themselves be trapped, when they should be masters of their own destiny, and not get carried away. He felt a sudden pride: he had loved Vera and had known some delightful times through her, but when he realised that she would destroy him, *he had had the courage to leave.* That was the beginning of his emancipation. Now he felt he was master of things. A poor soldier lost in a mass of others, but the humble curve of his back gave him, he felt, more spring to his step.

He went back to the tent.

'Hey, Perrin,' he called gaily. 'Aren't you cold? The wind is beginning to whip your face like a lash!'

'It's certainly not warm in your blasted *bled.*'

Perrin was looking serious. He had been thinking too, but quite different thoughts. He had been thinking that five years was a long time to drag out. And he had been looking at the countryside around, and thinking of other countries he had known.

'And you call this countryside!'

Orschanow smiled. He knew Perrin, and knew how he always started off by cursing and maligning any new place he came to, but soon adapted to it.

A thin, scrofulous lad came up to him, his hands in his

pockets and the peak of his kepi turned straight up to the sky.

'Well, well, wasn't there any grub back home, for you to come here? Aha! you're going to be sticking bully beef and tapeworms and *barbaque* as tough as my grandmother's ribs up your muskets!'

With his rough, Parisian accent he was obviously trying to shock the 'blues' and to enjoy their ignorance of African army slang. Perrin shrugged his shoulders. But Orschanow looked him in the eye and said: 'It's you who can't have had enough to eat, to look such a scruff! As for the rest of us, if you want to see what we're made of, you've only got to come over here. If you came here to show off, you've got it wrong. You're a "blue" like the rest of us.'

'What, me?'

A straggler, who had come over to them and heard the argument, agreed: 'Yes, the tall bloke's right. If you're not a blue, why are you in this dump?'

The ruffian looked at Orschanow's broad shoulders and slunk away.

Orschanow smiled. His time among the *bourlaki* had taught him how to deal with such people.

'Bless my soul, if we kick off with arguments, we're in for a bad time,' Perrin said, for although he was brave and strong, he hated quarrels and fights. 'And it's my opinion that there's a right bunch of beggars around here. We'll have to watch out! You know, in the army you're responsible for your own things. It's often a court-martial if anything's missing. So we'll have to watch out that no one pinches anything from us. We really let ourselves in for something when we joined up.'

'The die is cast, we have to get on with it.'

'Well, that's for sure. Good Lord! it's not the pawnshop

here. You can deliver your goods but you can't get them out again.' This made them laugh.

Orschanow knew that Perrin never gave up, never harboured grudges, and reduced everything to its simplest form. But this kind of wisdom doesn't come easily to intellectuals or to people with imagination, people who are always wanting to correct the balance. Certainly the reason for their flight was that he, Dmitri, had got scared. There was some cowardice in their action, in *his* action. He shouldn't have brought Perrin into it.

They lay in the cold tent, buffeted by the wind. Orschanow did not sleep. He was thinking that he was to blame for everything, because of his lack of will-power at the start of the strike, because he hadn't known how to secure his freedom by abstention, by not getting involved, because he had wanted to act with bravado, and hadn't even managed to carry that through properly.

*

The next morning, in the cold, bare hall in the barracks, the recruits were presented to the colonel, a thin, tall, greying man with piercing blue eyes and gruff gestures.

'What's your name?'

'Perrin, Antoine, sir.'

'Where d'you come from?'

'From Geneva, in Switzerland.'

'What did you do in civilian life?'

'I was a farm labourer, sir.'

'Why did you join up?'

'To serve France, sir.'

The officer gave him a blank, astonished stare as he heard the tremble in Perrin's voice. He passed on to Orschanow.

'There was no work, sir. I was cold and hungry, in Savoy, in Marseilles,' said Orschanow. The colonel peered at him.

'There are things which are known here because we're told them, and others which we're not told about. I haven't the right to press you about them. But there are matters which interest me from another point of view, and which could affect your ranking. They tell me you were a medical student before becoming a labourer. Why did you give it up?'

'Because I wanted to, sir.'

'Yes, it is after all your own affair. Here, with care, good conduct and above all with discipline, you could make a position for yourself. I am merciless about one thing: drunkenness, remember that.'

'I said it was to serve France,' Perrin said as they left, 'because you see it always gets me when I have to say I'm Swiss.'

2

That evening after supper they went on their first sortie into town, passing through the gateway under the strict eye of the sergeant at guard. They passed by the military hospital, dark and sombre against the red evening sun. The straight roads were lined with European-style houses, shops and avenues of scraggy plane trees and *faux-poivriers*.

'Just like a small town in the Midi,' Perrin said. But it was the motley crowd which really caught their attention: legionnaires, *Chasseurs d' Afrique*, Spanish workers wearing dull, neutral European clothes, and crowds of Arabs everywhere, in white or earth-coloured burnouses and tawny-tasseled turbans, with the occasional shepherd and a few women wearing woollen *haïks* and scurrying to and fro as if fleeing something. The nearer the two legionnaires got to the native quarter, the louder the lively hubbub became. In their open shops, Mozabites with impassive faces, large black beards and short djellabas sat like lords amongst their varied goods: green and fawn earthenware pots, basket-ware and mats of palm, sprigs or dried red pepper looking like clusters of coral. There were men from Tlemcen, with hooded black capes decorated with little pieces of brightly coloured cloth, Negroes, roadsweepers pushing their small donkeys in front of them, loaded porters running through the streets sweating. Outside the Moorish cafés, on benches and mats, natives bent their dry, fine profiles over games, while others savoured the sweet delight of feline immobility.

In front of the markets soldiers gathered in cliques, according to their regiment, with a continual clicking of sabres, bayonets and spurs. As the winter evening fell on this colourful scene, a clear pink light fell on the snowy mountain-tops and threw purple shadows in the small streets.

They went on past an empty, leprous, stubbly area where hardly a weed grew, into a maze of whitewashed houses with soldiers and women sprawling outside on white benches and mats. What a revelation these women in these African hovels were, all kinds of races, all kinds of costumes, all kinds of jewellery! There were Moors dressed in pointed tarbooshes and brilliant silks, dark-skinned Negresses in gaudy colours, Bedouins with expressionless, tattooed faces and haughty looks, like bronze idols. And then the girls from the south, above all from the mountain plateaux and the Djebel Amour, with high golden bonnets on their heads, or plaits of black hair and red wool, or silver coronets and bouquets of ostrich feathers. The Ouled-Naïl were the most heavily hung with jewellery, the metallic reflections of which danced on their silk and fine wool *mlahfas* wrapped around with ancient skill, in gorgeous colours. They wore little silver chains worked into their hair, large earrings, pieces of gold, coral and scented paste hanging from their heavy necklaces and belts, and thin or thick bracelets, riveted with nail-heads. Their ankles tinkled with the noise of perforated silver anklets. There were beautiful ones and repulsive ones, young, amber-skinned ones, and fat or faded ones. Some of them chattered as they drank coffee or absinthe, others smoked, with an air of fierce, dreamy independence.

Melancholy tunes rose into the air from tortoise-shell or reed pipes, and men's voices sang southern laments, with variations of tone or voice but with the same monotonous underlying chorus. Lanterns began to be lit in tiny bare rooms furnished with one miserable bed, or more simply still, with only a coarse Bedouin rug spread on the ground. A pungent smell hung all around, a mixture of rosewater, sweat, absinthe, and tobacco. The troops, let loose amongst this sensual showiness, howled with excitement and with a lust for pleasure, for relief and oblivion.

A hoarse cry interrupted by plaintive commands came from a place in the shadows – some Arabs trying to get their camels to kneel down.

Orschanow avidly drank in all this unknown world, whose splendour he could perceive beneath its rags and misery, but Perrin walked alongside him stupefied, his arms dangling.

'Let's stop for a coffee,' Orschanow said, so that he could sit on a mat and watch at his leisure a particular area which had caught his attention. Perrin hesitated and then sat gauchely on a bench, next to a Spahi who made way for him. Perrin said, 'Good evening everyone.' Only the Spahi and the women replied. Orschanow stretched out on the mat.

He was feeling the effects of his Muslim blood from his mother's Tatar ancestry, and felt good there, in the nonchalant position which he had often taken by the roadside. He didn't feel any awkwardness under the eyes of these men from a different world, who were surprised to see legionnaires, *roumis*, sitting companionably amongst them. The Muslims knew that they were viewed with contempt by the Europeans, and their response was one of absolute disdain, complete indifference to everything new which the *roumis* might bring to their silent country with its vast horizons.

'I must learn their language,' thought Dmitri, who always wanted to live the life of the people, wherever he was. He and Perrin still had no money, so they couldn't even think of the easy conquests displayed before their eyes. And anyway, Perrin wasn't tempted by all these foreigners, who terrified him. These women who kept brushing up against him, speaking French with a throaty accent, seemed to him more or less like ghosts. He didn't look at them, or reply to them, so they called out to him in German, thinking he didn't understand. Pressed too hard by one of them, a tall pale girl in a flowery *gandoura*, he finally replied sullenly: 'No use wasting your breath. I understand French, and everything else.'

Orschanow was amused, sensing that for his part he would come back here, sometimes just to lie and dream and sometimes to gratify a sudden lust, and he spoke to them gently, teasing them, asking their names, listening, as they started to speak Arabic among themselves, to their laughter and their strange gurgling language, with its jarring aspirates, even hoarser than those of Russian. They complimented him, told him he was good-looking. And he promised to come back, when he had money.

Perrin was bored, but since he could see that his friend wasn't going to move on, and was content, he didn't want to take him away. How the devil did this Russian manage to feel at home anywhere straight away?

Eventually, he got up.

'Do you want to come and have a drink over there?' he said, pointing to a Jewish hovel at the end of the road.

'No, I'm fine here, you know me. You go on . . . we'll meet up later.'

Orschanow was grateful to Perrin for his instinctive tact, for never trying to impose his own tastes on him, or to oppose his sudden needs for solitude, silence or wandering. He went off to find more accessible pleasures, discreetly, without any resentment, leaving Orschanow to cope on his own, as he put it.

And Dmitri stayed there stretched out on the mat until the evening call, in no hurry to penetrate this new life, living it to the full already, happy from the first moment he had arrived.

3

A blue and white pottery stove stood in the narrow bar, its door shaped like a Moorish arch, and with small, naively-decorated mugs and polished copper plates and coffee-pots lined up on the steps at its side. A few native customers sat on benches in the room, and the owner, a tall, tanned Moroccan, was making coffee on the stove with slow, confident movements. He wore a long, brown linen blouse and a small white turban around his bright red fez.

Orschanow was crouched in a corner on a mat next to a young Arab with soft black eyes and a downy beard around his fleshy lips. When he laughed, he looked very gentle, like a child. He was dictating Arabic words to Orschanow, who copied them down in Russian letters. Orschanow had discovered a willing teacher, who spoke good French and was delighted with this *roumi*'s enthusiasm to learn his language. When Orschanow had told him about his mother's Muslim ancestry, his surprise had turned to friendliness. His name was Mohammed, and he had been a Spahi, but he was the son of a poor Koranic teacher and was therefore well educated in Arabic.

'Come and have some soup with us tomorrow,' he said to Orschanow.

'Are you married?'

'No, but I've a woman from the Negro part of town who will come and make a couscous for us. Promise you'll come?'

'Definitely. Come and collect me from the barracks at five.'

'I haven't many friends, you know, because I'm too proud and too civilised. If you don't want people to look down on you here, you must keep your mouth shut and be cunning. I'll show you everything you need to know. You don't need anyone else, you can trust me.'

The next day the Arab came at five to collect his friend. Orschanow's fellow soldiers raised their eyes a little at this unconventional friendship between a legionnaire and a native. But Orschanow kept apart from them, engrossed in his new experiences.

Perrin confided with a smile that in the evening he had arranged to meet a Spanish woman who had taken his fancy. Native life still unnerved and even repelled him – it was so alarmingly different – and he continued to be wary of these people of another race.

*

In a small, crumbling, whitewashed house, its walls lined with shaky boards, a green and yellow rug was laid out, patterned with flowers. Calico-covered cushions were propped against the wall instead of chairs. On the floor was a copper lamp and a gaudily-painted chest with old ironwork on it. A Moorish girl wearing a white *mlahfa* greeted the men with a tired face, kissing their hands. Little bells hung from her bracelets and anklets, and her forehead was tattooed like the Bedouins'. Her voice was slow, a little hoarse, tender.

'We're going to drink some absinthe,' Mohammed said. 'The woman will serve us.'

And, indeed, she didn't sit down beside them, but kept to her assumed role of wife, attentively obeying the former Spahi as he acted master of the house. Some glasses, a carafe of water and a bottle of Pernod appeared on the rug.

'Did you start drinking in the army?' Orschanow asked him.

'Yes, in the army – it ruins people. Before, all I did was smoke, but now I swear like a trooper, I drink absinthe and I eat pork – and long may it last, my friend!' He leant back against the cushions, and winked at the legionnaire. 'Don't worry, later on Zohra's sister will be coming.'

Orschanow relaxed in this warm, scented atmosphere, his throat beginning to burn from the drink. Zohra, who was standing, looked at them with a laugh.

'Si Mohammed, should I bring the supper?' she said.

'Bring it in.'

As they ate the highly spiced and scented food from one plate, there was a knock at the door. It was Aïcha, a dark, frail girl with that fierce, impenetrable Bedouin look in her eye which Orschanow had already noticed and found disturbing. She seemed to him very beautiful, with her dark blue veils covered with silver baubles. She was younger than Zohra: her face, with tattoos on the forehead, had the freshness of wild flowers. She sat silently in the corner, as still as an idol. She wore a silver diadem, its little coral pendants dropping down from her dark hair. She lowered her eyes, not even looking at this *roumi* for whose benefit her sister had told her to come.

Zohra was more forthcoming, and, seeing that Mohammed was a little drunk, slipped towards him across the floor.

'Some absinthe, for heaven's sake!' Smiling, he flung her down onto the rug.

'Why are you hurting her?' Orschanow said, trying to stop him.

'That's nothing. If you saw how I beat her when I feel like it, when I'm angry! She likes it. Hey, you like it, don't you?'

She nodded her head in agreement, for fear of being beaten again. Mohammed magnanimously gave her a drink and a cigarette.

'Aïcha, come here, come and drink, don't be ashamed,' Zohra said. But her sister, only just out of her village, wouldn't move.

Mohammed nudged his companion: 'She's ashamed.'

Orschanow's head was spinning. This atmosphere of brutality didn't displease him. How he had despised himself, long ago, for the taste he knew he had for violent love-making, and which had often driven him to actions he was ashamed of. Now he abandoned himself to it calmly, consciously, in spite of his intoxication.

Mohammed was telling him about Aïcha. She had been married off, but had a haughty, wilful character which her husband had never been able to control, and she had run off to join her sister.

'They're often like that, Bedouins. You have to know how to handle them.'

Orschanow allowed himself to go along with the savage high spirits of the Arab, who was fighting with Zohra now, rolling her along the ground with one hand, like a ball. As always, these wrestling games attracted him and finished up by driving him wild.

He got up, his northern capacity for alcohol keeping him steady on his feet. He took Aïcha, lifting her up to his mouth in spite of her young cat's nails which dug into his wrists, threw her onto the cushions and, suddenly seized with an irresistible, animal need to violate her, forced her to drink a glass of absinthe. She stiffened to escape him, turning her head away, clenching her teeth. But she had to drink, Orschanow's hand on her throat, as his eyes flashed.

Suddenly the candle went out, pushed by Mohammed's foot, and everything rocked in drunkenness and darkness.

4

It was snowing and a freezing wind swept the deserted streets. Orschanow, not yet sober, was running so that he could get back before the rollcall. Mohammed, with his old soldier's *sangfroid*, had had to push him out. Dmitri had forgotten about everything in the excitement of his savage consummation.

Now, in the intense cold, he was dizzy and fevered. He got back just in time, as the bugle was sounding its shrill note.

'For God's sake,' Perrin said, 'you're really drunk!'

'Yes, I'm drunk. God damn this job, where you have to leave everything to come back at bedtime like a kid!'

Perrin carefully picked up the clothes which Orschanow had thrown off haphazardly, and which gave off a strong odour. He knew his friend, and the sudden raging lusts he was prey to. This fury had always astonished him, as someone who liked a bit of fun but never lost his self-possession. He didn't understand the passions of the man from the steppes, who had something primitive underneath his veneer of education, while he, the simple workman, had generations and generations of peaceful, stolid peasants behind him.

'You've got excited over a woman again!' he said, seeing Orschanow curled up on his bed, his eyes dark and fiery.

And so the ex-medical student had become, after all, just like the common men he had chosen to live among. He had even surpassed them, at least those from Europe, in approaching man's original savagery. Orschanow didn't regret anything, didn't despise himself any more. At times, after he had left Geneva, he had examined himself, fearing that these sudden, almost murderous lusts were a symptom of some neurosis. But no, they corresponded to the most joyous times in his life, days of health and energy. Under their sway, his faculties were heightened, he lived fully, felt happy and in love with life once more. And they had calmed him down. Anyway, no thoughts of unnatural or morbid sensuality had ever entered into these rages. That was just the way he was, and the knowledge of his simple virility, renewed at its source, gave him hours of happiness. Why then was he to be tormented by complex scruples from now on?

*

He listened vaguely to the chaotic Babel of conversation going on around him, deep voices joking in different languages, arguments inside the frail tents buffeted by the wind. His place was here now. He would curl up here, make a niche for himself amongst these companions, each of whom had his own secret past. All these lads had had cruel and damaging things happen to them, and now they were blotting them out, escaping. They had abandoned for a while their cumbersome personalities, as if they were shedding a garment that was too restrictive, and assuming another that enabled them to walk more at ease, to live a freer inner life under the tyranny of rules, relieved of the dead weight of responsibility. In this return to the warmth of the herd, to animal life, there was a sense of relief at casting off a burden, a lightening of the chest.

To unearth the sense of an intact and timeless personality, to find hidden embers under dead ashes, the sense of eternities of instinct . . : Orschanow felt all this, lying in his tent like a contented animal, and pictured the miserable Saïda, the refuge of damaged hearts, with delight.

5

Orschanow was robust and supple, and his training as a recruit was progressing well under the direction of the irascible and ruddy-faced Sergeant Schmütz, who barked and swore constantly through his ginger whiskers. Orschanow had managed to win him over by speaking German to him and by working hard. For him the sheer, healthy physical exhaustion which made him collapse into bed each night redeemed the stupidity and pointlessness of military life. He liked best of all the lowly job of guard, or the hours spent in the small courtyard on sunny days brushing his thick linen uniform and dungarees. The legionnaires would sing laments from their own countries, adding an exotic touch to this drab little area between the courtyard and the 'Senegal', the punishment barracks which were the scourge of the less disciplined recruits.

The days passed, filled with futile routine and drudgery, but the morning always held the pleasant prospect of four hours of liberty in the evening. The legionnaires were almost all good soldiers, particularly on forced marches. And yet there were hardly any who really liked their profession. The majority preferred skiving and malingering. The deliberately hard discipline weighed heavily on them, and the punishment barracks were never empty; in the courtyard every day you could see a wan, bad-tempered, inwardly seething group paying for their misdemeanours, carrying heavy sacks, sometimes full of stones. Some of the sergeants took a sadistic pleasure in making the men do the most painful and drawn-out exercises possible. Sergeant Schmütz's specialities, for example, were non-stop gymnastics in summer and getting the men to hold long, freezing poses in winter. All those who didn't obey, and there were many of them, were punished or court-martialled. After enduring all forms of punishment in the 'correction cells', they were confined to barracks for 'disciplining'. Some proudly described themselves as 'indestructible'.

One of them, a Breton who drank like a fish and who had once been a quartermaster in the navy, used to say cryptically in the barrack-room: 'You know what I long for? To be *done in*.' One day when the squadron corporal made some remark to him, he ferociously split the man's skull open with the butt-end of his musket. When they took him away to the cells he said, 'You see, I meant what I said. Now I'm going to be *done in*.' Shortly afterwards the legionnaires heard that he had been condemned to death. They took the news with their customary indifference towards their comrades' fates.

Dmitri felt a sympathy for these rebels who admitted defeat in advance but still refused to bow their heads, and he suddenly recalled Orlow, the *brodiaga* who had burned the village of Neoplatimowka to take his revenge on an innkeeper. It was true that Orschanow had never discovered the epic, heroic side of the Legion which had attracted him as a child-rebel in the steppes, but it seemed to him that these men had their own grandeur all the same.

'Cretins!' said Perrin. 'Why get into trouble when you're not in a strong position? It doesn't help matters at all.' He thought you should try to live well wherever you were, and that it was stupid to want to break your neck when you could quite respectably give way.

'I'm not saying that if they made us do abominable things we shouldn't protest, because yes, at that point we'd have the right to. But what are they asking us to do here? To obey and to do the work which we signed up to do. It's only fair. If I sign on for haymaking, then I must stay until the end of haymaking. It's only right, and here it's the same thing.'

6

Every evening Orschanow savoured to the full the daily revelation of oriental life, in Moorish cafés, at Zohra's house, or in the other whitewashed houses of the Negro part of town. After four months, he could speak Arabic reasonably fluently, and could join in interminable, slow discussions, which had the resonance and richness of music to him, outside the cafés. The Arab world, so closed to him at first, was opening up bit by bit, and Orschanow, the refugee occidental, was beginning to merge into the colourful, perfumed background. In the native areas, which were the only ones he enjoyed, they were getting used to him.

'What a pity you're a *roumi*!' said Mohammed, who now loved him like a brother.

'But I'm not a *roumi*,' Orschanow objected, smiling. 'I don't come from any religion, and if I had to choose one it would be Islam.' And indeed Islam had enveloped him in its melancholy charm, its solace and serenity. Faced with bad fortune and death, the Arab remained impassive, unresisting, almost unaffected, and this appealed to all Orschanow's hereditary fatalism, and drew him to these men. Wasn't he their spiritual brother? Hadn't he voluntarily renounced the battle for life and work, the aim of all European life, in order to let himself be carried along as they were, drifting deliciously on the tide of life? And then, he was a nomad, an inveterate vagabond. Other traits linked the Muslims to the Russian people, a people Orschanow still loved with a deep and agonising love. Like the Russian people, the Arab races survived by the force of an almost unchangeable inertia. Like them, they suffered in silence, bringing the same resignation, the same submission, the same tacit reproval of injustice to any dealings they had with the authorities. The Russian said: 'My birth decreed it.' The Arab, more laconic, contented himself with making a vague gesture of submission and saying: '*Mektoub* – it was written!'

Orschanow recognised certain touching Slavonic customs amongst the Arabs – their cult of hospitality, their generosity and their charity towards the poor. They were melancholic, unable to understand the frivolous occidental gaiety which was so foreign to Orschanow's mentality. They had their moments of light-hearted joy, their own childish laughter, but they would immediately fall back into gravity, and retire into themselves. Most of the time they were content simply to smile.

In addition, like the ordinary Slavs, they were sociable and egalitarian, and showed no disdain for the poor. The rich and the lettered would sit side by side with the most wretched, in the great brotherhood of Islam. If a beggar came into a café, people would make room for him, and exchange the same salutations of peace as they would with any Muslim. So Orschanow slipped happily into the indolent, uncomplicated contentment of Arab life.

Mohammed, who was a kef-smoker, persuaded Dmitri to give up alcohol in favour of the little pipe filled with hemp-dust. So, instead of the boisterous intoxication of drink, Dmitri got to know the sweet torpor of kef, an infinite peace which descended as the yellowish smoke rose into the warm air.

7

Behind a Moorish café, in a small whitewashed courtyard tinged with blue, an ancient vine had twined around a gnarled fig tree in reclusive camaraderie. A dry-stone wall formed a kind of circular bench around a narrow well. In the odd niche in the walls were lodged pots of basil or jugs stuffed with sprigs of lentisk. A jasmine grew in an old box, its pink and white flowers dropping intermittently onto the mats beneath. A falcon sat dreaming, tethered to its perch, and nightingales dozed in little cages made of porcupine quills.

This was the clandestine kef-smoking den run by Hadj Adda, an educated, serious and courteous Moroccan Negro. His white-bearded, ebony face smiled at the regulars whenever he accepted their offer of a small pipe of kef. From five o'clock onwards the small garden began to come to life. Some twenty people gathered there, street-porters, Bedouins passing through, Moors. There was nothing orgiastic about these meetings. The men smoked kef without speaking much to each other, and then there would be Arab music and song. You would never find a woman there, or hear a coarse joke. This sensual pleasure was enough in itself.

*

Mohammed had introduced Orschanow to the place, vouching for this legionnaire at whom they'd looked askance to start with. But soon they got used to him, treating him as a brother, smiling at him when he arrived.

He stretched out next to the former Spahi and listened, pipe in hand and with his eyes half-closed, to the soft twittering of the captive nightingales and the dream-like music of the *hacheïchia*, the kef-smokers.

Mohammed was playing the *djouak*, drawing muted strains, sometimes languid, sometimes with an almost unearthly sadness, out of this bit of reed which he'd got from the bottom of a *wadi*.

Hammou Benhalima, a porter in European rags, with a blue cotton scarf rolled around his tarboosh, was playing a Spanish guitar. An old man with a clean-shaven, impassive face, his eyes closed as if dreaming, scraped on an old violin which he had on his knee, Arab-fashion. A group of Bedouins with thin bird-of-prey profiles and chestnut eyes under the hooded veils of their tawny-tasselled turbans slid pieces of bark along the two strings of their *guibri*, threw back their heads and closed their eyes. The ecstatic *hacheïchia* were singing. Sometimes they sang Bedouin dirges, epics of hunting, love and battle; sometimes maraboutic songs, *Borda*, in honour of the Prophet; sometimes songs of passionate, doomed love, full of bleeding hearts, which distilled drop by drop the burning tears wrought by separation and forgetfulness.

In the flickering candlelight, Orschanow, roused from his semi-oblivion, watched the groups with their lithe, feline contours, as they crouched or lay, and the expressions on their faces, which gradually grew paler and more spiritual with the inebriation of the song, the music and the kef. The citizens were sinking voluptuously into ecstasy; the Bedouins' bronze faces, however, were still ferociously grave, except that their pupils shone a little more brilliantly under their slightly more hooded eyes.

People said very little, and Hadj Adda silently handed round little cups of coffee, or tiny glasses of Moroccan tea with peppery mint.

8

It was night-time, and in the dark a sigh of lassitude seemed to rise from the men's sleeping-quarters. Bodies arched and sweated in the coarse brown sheets, and now and then a groan or a cough broke the silence. Sunk in the dreamless sleep of childhood, Orschanow had thrown off his sheets, and his bare arms hung out of the bed. Suddenly he started, as a harsh noise awoke him. A bugle was being blown in the courtyard, its call sounding slow, strange and lugubrious to Orschanow through his sleepy torpor. Corporal Vialar was already up, crying 'Everyone awake! Alert!' and the legionnaires were falling out of bed pell-mell, cursing, half-asleep. For a moment Dmitri thought there must have been some catastrophe.

'It's another bloody crackpot idea of the colonel's — to

get everyone used to leaping around in the middle of the night.'

In the town the infantry's trumpet repeated the call, then a cannon blasted through the darkness and silence of the sleeping town. The corporal lit a lamp. With a clicking of swords and a noise of leather belts hurriedly buckled, everyone got dressed, with much cursing and grumbling. On the staircases the boots of the other squads began clattering down the steps.

'Come on, for God's sake! You bunch of layabouts, jump to it!' Sergeant Schmütz bellowed, pale and still not quite sober from the night before.

In the courtyard, lanterns filed along like will o' the wisps, casting sudden pools of red light onto the trees. The sections began to line up, with a rattle of metal and the clack and stamp of studded boots. Alerted by a sergeant, the officers were arriving. Lieutenant Clerc was buttoning up his collar, with clenched teeth and a flicker of anger in his eyes: he had had to desert a bird of passage, a delicious Belgian girl, in a hotel in the town.

Finally the colonel arrived on his huge white horse. Cold and erect as if for a review of troops, he asked if everything was in order. Suddenly, terse orders were shouted, and they all left, turning on the road towards the south. In the darkness all that could be heard was the thud of marching boots and the occasional clash of steel.

*

They climbed laboriously up steep stony slopes, at a rapid pace. 'We're going to Aïn-el-Hadjar!' one legionnaire murmured. Goaded on by the NCOs, they marched on, their hearts full of rancour at their impotence in the face of the

142

tedium and hardship of this futile servitude. Only Orschanow among them was not bored. For the first time he
was seeing the Bedouin countryside clearly, in the vague
half-light of the spring night. The shrubs took on a gro-
tesque look, seeming to move around, black and confused.
The *wadis* opened up, apparently bottomless, and the tops
of the mountains were etched crisply against the dull pallor
of the horizon. Once or twice, in the thickly glittering sky,
a star would detach itself like a ripe fruit and fall into
infinity. In the silence of the mountains you could hear a
powerful life-force beating, the prodigious birth of the
African spring. Jackals howled, running in packs on the
hills.

*

The legionnaires arrived, breathless, at the huge plateau of
Aïn-el-Hadjar. There, beyond the sea of alfalfa rustling in
the warm wind, the horizon opened out, vast, immense,
free. Orschanow felt a great sense of relief: at last, no more
oppressive mountains, no more walls to block the sky. He
happily breathed in the light air of this altitude. His love
of the African country deepened: suddenly he didn't feel
an exile any more, and longed just to stay here forever, in
this stark landscape, even if it could only be in the lowly
blue cap of the legionnaire.

Slowly the horizon lightened, as a diffuse, greenish light
traced around the lacy mountain peaks, muting the uniform
blackness of the night to reveal the opaque silhouettes
of lentisk bushes and dwarf palms. Through the surging,
closely-knit alfalfa, the plateau appeared flecked like a
panther's skin. Then the light grew brighter, the sun rose
in the sky, and the legionnaires were no longer a dark,

amorphous mass. A light breeze blew through the leathery grasses, softly brushing against faces covered in red dust and sweat. To Dmitri this joyful experience of dawn in the open air was his favourite moment, as hope and life were renewed with the coming of the benevolent light.

A troop of men was approaching sombrely through the sea of alfalfa. In the lilac morning light, the men, dressed in blue jackets and kepis with enormous square peaks, and with shaved, emaciated faces and hollow, dull eyes, filed past between the legionnaires with their bayonets fixed, and military police guards with their revolvers at their sides. They were the *Pégriots*, the prisoners from Aïn-el-Hadjar, on their way to work, their tools over their shoulders. Some of the dark-skinned ones, their foreheads and hands tattooed, retained their Arab gravity under their convicts' clothes. Other, fairer ones, whose hair looked bleached against their burnt skin, exchanged looks with the passing soldiers: they had been legionnaires themselves, and were now convicts, and they looked at their former comrades without a smile, and with the hatred of slaves for *the others*, those from the outside, who seemed to them free men. The sad helots tramped past, resigned as a herd of cattle, oblivious to the glory of the rising sun, in a world of red mists swirling above the melancholy plain.

Under his heavy soldier's harness, Orschanow felt revolt stirring in him, as he perceived all the *conventions*, all the lies of civilised life: the lie at the base of a society which arrogates to itself a right which it denies to individuals, the right to renew ancient slaveries, and to bring its whole weight to bear against those who do not want to conform to it.

Oh! to be able to go off into the bush, to live alone, in your own way, without knuckling under to these illusory and imbecilic ideas which crushed men with their harsh tyranny. Orschanow's vagabond instincts were rebelling again, as he realised he still had some four years of service to live out amongst men, under their authority and their threats! But he had to pull himself together and wait, march blindly and dumbly, seizing moments of real life where he could, like the intoxicating sight of this dawn in the desert.

9

There was a legionnaire called Pedro Garcia in Corporal Vialar's squad who kept himself apart from the others, lost in his own dark thoughts. He was tall and wiry, and his hair was very black and curly under his red and black kepi. The angles of his bronzed face were ridged with copper highlights, and a thin moustache etched his sensual lips, which never smiled, and were always closed.

From the very first day, everyone had put two and two together from the scraps of information he had given the corporal. Of course, it wasn't true, they didn't believe he was a Spanish deserter. They instantly christened him with a nickname which made him blanch: the *Bicot*, that is, 'the Arab'.

He and Orschanow slept next to each other. The *Bicot* didn't talk to Orschanow any more than he did to the others, but he treated him differently, since he appreciated the fact that he respected his silence, and didn't scoff at him. Vialar had often had to intervene to silence the jibes of the others: 'For heaven's sake, give that man some peace!

145

What does it matter to you whether he's Arab or Spanish? No doubt all of you lot scrupulously gave your real name and real nationality when *you* joined up, didn't you?'

'That's true, Corporal, you're right,' Perrin sighed, still regretting that he'd had to call himself Swiss.

When the legionnaires were camping out once on the plateau of Aïn-el-Hadjar the *Bicot* had happened to help Orschanow out in a small way. He was an excellent soldier, as clean as a cat, always washing his things and polishing his leathers. He had none of the clumsiness of the 'new blue' which he should have been, seeing that he'd joined up barely three months before.

'Why didn't you ever go out in Saïda?' Dmitri asked him.

'I don't like larking around.'

'Well, let's go out together. I shan't ask you any questions, and you needn't tell me anything if you don't want to. I'm not interested in knowing things which don't concern me.'

'When you go out, where do you go in Saïda?'

'I go to the Moorish café, or for walks along the road.'

'That's an idea, it's interesting out on the road.'

That evening they walked for a long time around the camp in the rose-tinted glory of the sun as it set over the vast, alluring horizon of the south.

'Where do you come from, then?' the *Bicot* asked.

'I'm Russian, through my father, and Tatar, through my mother. And you?'

'Me? ... You know how I said I was called Pedro Garcia ... well, it's not true. The others are right. But why shouldn't I tell you? I come from Bou-Saada, and my name is Lamri Belhaouari.'

And he told him his life story, as if to justify himself.

He was the son of a *cadi*, the local Muslim magistrate. He had gone to the local French-Arab school, then on to college in Algiers. Being rich, he had never needed to work. When he had returned to Bou-Saada, his father had given him a delightful little house in gardens bordering the *wadi*. He had married him to a young and very pretty second cousin of his, Halima.

Lamri had fallen in love with his young wife. One evening someone came to tell him his father had fallen ill, and he had reluctantly left his peaceful house and his Halima and run over to his father's, saying he would be back the next day. But the old man had already recovered, and Lamri happily returned to his own house. He had a key, and slipped in quietly. There, in the cool air of the courtyard where they used to sleep in the summer-time, he had found Halima in the arms of one of his cousins, Ali. Lamri went crazy. He massacred the lovers with a knife, and then, hurling himself across them, steeped in their blood, he had lain there prostrate and unconscious until dawn. He was arrested, and the court-martial which had tried him, since he was a native in military territory, had given him only two years in prison.

In the penal colony of Berrouaghia, Lamri had lived out his two years in a dark dream. His father was dead, and Bou-Saada seemed to him empty and desolate when he returned. So, leaving all his worldly goods to his brother Ahmed, the *cadi*'s assistant, he had joined the Spahis, out of boredom. Towards the end of his fourth year with them he had been drafted to Aumale, where he had fallen in love with a beautiful Jewish woman. One evening, as luck would have it, he had quarrelled with another Spahi at this woman's house. They had come to blows, and Lamri had wounded his friend. For the second time he was

147

court-martialled, and was condemned to one year in prison, the court having admitted an element of provocation.

When he got out of prison, Lamri, tired of life and despairing of ever being anything but an outcast, finished the four months of service he still had to do. Then, in order to disappear forever and forget everything, he had come and joined the Legion under a false name.

'It's all over for me now,' he concluded. 'I don't live, I just dream, and God knows my dreams are black.' He was very intelligent, and although he was usually so quiet he had spoken clearly and evocatively, in perfect French.

'Keep what I've told you to yourself. As for you, you're still young. Try not to do what I've done.'

10

By the time Orschanow's five years in the Legion were drawing to an end, his own philosophy had grown close to the *Bicot*'s: his aim was to create a sealed, personal world of his own, wrapped around with dreams, keeping any hostile intrusion from outside at arm's length, and only to see the people and to feel the things which he chose to see and feel. In the monotonous, restricted life of the Legion, where he was sheltered from the fight to win a daily living, Orschanow had pretty well managed to put his programme of aesthetic egoism into practice.

But his time in the Legion was nearly over, and the pressing question of the immediate future was forcing him to confront realities he wanted to avoid. He had, however, grown a little wiser, and he tried to force himself to reason calmly and to avoid an impulsive decision. The painful anxiety which had plagued him for years, giving him a disproportionate need for action, and which was exacerbated by his inability to satisfy this need, had yielded to a great calm, and to an entirely reflective turn of mind. On the face of it, he was almost never alone. Perpetually surrounded by noisy, demanding individuals with the spiteful, shallow turn of mind which comes from constant superficial contact with other people, Orschanow had come to live like a real anchorite. His life had become a contemplative dream, from the moment when he understood – or thought he understood – that we carry our happiness within us, and that what we're searching for in the changing mirror of external life is our own image.

But now he had to resolve this urgent question: would he stay, would he prolong, for another five years, until he was thirty-six and his youth was over, this slow-paced life which he enjoyed, or would he set off now, free, regenerated, and delivered from his old craziness? His reason told him that he didn't need to stay any longer. He had got his naturalisation, because the powers that be had taken an interest in him. This meant that he could stay in this country which he loved, and make Algeria his adoptive home. His soul had come out victorious and fortified from all his difficulties. He had found the secret of happiness. Once again he felt an intense need for freedom and the wandering life.

*

After supper one evening at the local soldiers' café some drunken Germans were banging their fists on the sticky marble table tops, and singing at the tops of their voices, only breaking off to argue. Two Czech students, who had arrived as apprentice corporals, and who had got Dmitri to come into this café with them, were discussing socialist theories. Orschanow wasn't listening to them, but was brooding, head in hands, on what to do. If he wanted to join up again he had one more day to do it. The heat and the noise of the place were becoming intolerable. The Germans got up, elbowing Dmitri and the Czechs on the pretext of wanting to drink with them. For the first time in several years, Dmitri was aware of the ugliness of his surroundings, and left abruptly.

On the white road outside the town some Bedouins, their ragged clothes purple in the rays of the setting sun, were singing mournfully as they drove their laden camels along. In front of them, at the top of a long, low hill, the road seemed to end, as the immense, golden horizon opened up. Freedom was good, and life was welcoming and exquisite to those who knew how to love and understand it. Dmitri had made his decision: he would leave, expand his dream, and, as a lover and an aesthete, possess life, which was proffering itself so generously.

*

'Adieu, Sergeant Schmütz!'

'Adieu, *der Russe*!' the subaltern said, giving a long, pensive, possibly envious look at the soldier who was going off forever, a free man.

The day was clear and fine. The bad winter weather was over, and the sun was already hot in the watery blue sky.

Dmitri's heart swelled with pleasure at the freedom he had finally gained. Gladly, and without bitterness, he set out from the barracks where he had suffered so much, and where his soul had been restored.

I I

Orschanow went from farm to farm, working for the colonials. He found them very different from the French peasants and often looked back wistfully on the times when he'd shared the rough lives of the good-hearted Savoyards. But he loved this stark, splendid country, and didn't want to leave it.

After the winter's work had ended, Dmitri stayed on as a permanent labourer with M. Moret, since the farmer was satisfied with this quiet, conscientious workman, who was content with a very modest salary, not much more than a native's. M. Moret's large farm was situated among eucalyptus and pepper-plants on the brow of a low hill overlooking the Mitidja plain. In the blue distance was the great massif of Ourarsenis, and Orleansville dominated the sinuous, furrowed valley of the Cheliff, its ramparts overflowing with gardens.

Dmitri had built himself a *gourbi* some way from the farm, on the banks of the dry river bed, thick with oleanders. Hay stacks, brown from the winter, masked the farm-house and buildings from view, and he had planted a few eucalyptus trees to give himself some privacy. The primitive hut became a real home for him, and he settled into a new life which was peaceful and uncomplicated, in spite of everything that was artificial and contrived about it.

To Dmitri material deprivation seemed one of the conditions of his freedom, and for a long time now he had not even bought books or papers, contenting himself, in his own phrase, with reading beauty in the great book of the universe which was open wide in front of him.

In this way, Orschanow had succeeded in living according to his philosophy, the aim of which was to master himself and his circumstances. He still did not understand that, if he had arrived at this state, it was only because circumstances hadn't been against him, nor that his power over them was an illusion.

*

Tatani, Mme Moret's servant, was a young, slender, dark-haired girl, with large wide-set eyes. She had a small mouth, and a sweet and graceful smile. She wore the costume of the Moorish townswomen, with a handkerchief knotted behind her head under her parting, a *gandoura* belted with a scarf, and a white blouse with puffed sleeves. Although she was already sixteen, she didn't wear the Muslim veil. This costume, so similar to that of the peasant girls from his home country, perhaps provoked a feeling which unexpectedly began to grow in Dmitri. Knowing the Russian *moujiks*, he loved the Bedouins, who were so like them — with the same profound lack of knowledge, but the same naive and unshakeable faith in a benevolent God and in an afterlife, where the justice which was absent from this world would reign. They were as poor, as miserable, and had the same passive resignation in face of the all-powerful authority which was mistress of their fate. Faced with injustice, they capitulated to it with the same fatalism. Tatani, the orphan servant, seemed to him the charming epitome of her race, and at first he felt a simple aesthetic pleasure in seeing her come and go in the courtyard or at home, so gracious, so alert. But Tatani smiled at Dmitri whenever she saw him. This handsome young man, of a type she was unfamiliar with, with rather long and wavy brown hair and large, grey, gentle and thoughtful eyes, had attracted the young servant. She had just lost her old aunt, who had brought her up strictly and well so that she wasn't cheeky like most of the Moorish servants. She was close to nature, spontaneous and uncomplicated. She had learnt about love-making early on, and felt a pleasurable confusion in Dmitri's presence. When he wasn't there, she thought quite unashamedly about how good it would be to be his.

The portly Mme Moret, although not an unpleasant woman, sincerely regarded the natives as an inferior race. She was demanding towards Tatani and often ill-treated her, sometimes even beating her, and Dmitri felt an increasing tenderness and pity towards the girl. Soon he started to question her about her family. Tatani only had one brother left, a workman in Ténès, who didn't bother about her and whom she no longer thought about. Dmitri was now celibate from choice, and for a long time he didn't even think about the possibility of taking Tatani as a lover. He simply enjoyed the servant's company with a clear conscience. But then a day came when he realised that she was no longer just a graceful vision embellishing his life, but that he shared the feeling which disturbed Tatani when they were together.

Yet since there was nothing bad or perverse in the new-found feeling, and since it felt delightful, Dmitri gave in to it. Tatani, already less shy, was beginning to question him in her turn. She spoke a little French, and by now Dmitri was familiar with Arabic. Tatani listened thoughtfully, but with astonishment, to his stories.

'Look at what God's Fate has done,' she said to him one day. 'You were born far, far away, so far that I don't even know where it might be, the place you're telling me about, because it seems another world to me. And then God brought you here, near to me who knows nothing and has never been further than Elasnam [Orléansville] or Ténès!' Sometimes Tatani had moments of wistfulness which Dmitri found ravishing. In spite of all the childlike simplicity of this girl's character, a veil of mystery surrounded this daughter of another race, adding to her attractions.

Since he was acting in good faith, Dmitri didn't reproach himself for entertaining an enticing idea: to make Tatani his love, his mistress. Weren't they free to love each other, beyond all human barriers, all artificial and hypocritical morals?

*

The red sun was setting behind the mountains which dominate the Mediterranean from Ténès to Mostaganem, its oblique rays rolling a wave of fire over the Medjadja. The few trees and buildings of the Morets' farm seemed magnified, surrounded by an aureole of purple cloud. In the fields the men's work had finished for the day, and there was silence.

Dmitri and Tatani were sitting hand in hand behind the shelter of the hay stacks without saying a word, because words would have spoilt the intense sweetness of the moment. Before she finally left to go back to the farm, Tatani softly promised Dmitri that she would come and join him that night in his *gourbi*. Once he was alone, Dmitri felt

154

amazed that happiness had come into his life like this, so simply, so unexpectedly. Now love's peace and intoxicating charm were being handed so generously to him, and he thought gratefully of his five years of moral hard labour down in Saïda ... Saïda! 'the blessed town', as it was known – yes, it was indeed blessed, that small, lost town, where, amidst the *Heimatlos*, ground down by the harshness of the world, he had learned to be happy!

12

From now on Dmitri Orschanow's life with the little Bedouin servant was a delightful dream. Almost every night she joined him in the darkness of his *gourbi*, tidying his humble workman's hut like a wife. Then, in the security of their love and the silence of the night, they told each other over and over again the childish, eternally consoling words of love.

What would their future be? They didn't think about it, except to imagine it as the indefinite continuation of their happiness, which, it seemed to them, ought to last for the rest of their lives. Yet between their two very different souls there remained a chasm of mystery. Dmitri saw Tatani as quite simple, scarcely more complicated than the birds of the plain. But this little bird, who laughed and hopped, was not at all like the creatures from the far-off northern lands where Dmitri had been born: in her was all the secular legacy of the Semitic race, dormant in the benevolent African landscape, in the melancholy shadow of Islam. To Tatani, Dmitri was an enigma: she loved him as intensely as she could love, whilst regretting that he was a *kefer*, an infidel. And yet, instinctively, she guessed that he was very knowledgeable. He knew the answers to all her questions. One day she said to him admiringly, 'You're very learned. You know everything.' Then, after a short silence, she added sadly, 'Yes, you know everything, except one thing which even I know, as ignorant as I am.'

'And what's that?'

'That there is only one God, and that Mohammed is his prophet.'

After mentioning the venerable name of *Nabi*, she added piously: 'May peace and health be with him!'

Dmitri took her hands: 'Tatani my love,' he said, 'it's true, I'm not a Muslim . . . But I'm not a Christian either, because if I had the good fortune to believe in God, I would certainly believe in him in the Muslim fashion.'

Tatani remained baffled. She didn't understand why, if he wasn't a *roumi*, Dmitri didn't become a Muslim, since she did not understand that a person could not believe in God.

All through the summer and for two months of autumn their happiness lasted untroubled. But one day the brother who had abandoned Tatani and whom she had forgotten came to the farm to collect his sister, as he had promised her in marriage. She tried to protest, but the law of the land was against her and she had to obey. Without even being able to see Dmitri, she had to veil her weeping face, and, mounted on a slow mule, to follow her brother to a nearby village where his wife's parents lived. She was received almost with contempt.

'You're lucky that an honest man wants to marry you, since you've come down so much in the world, being the servant of a *roumi*, whom all the world has seen debauching herself with workmen.' This was how her brother spoke to her. Tatani had been given to Ben-Ziane, an Arab tenant-farmer of M. Moret's, so she came back to live on the farm estate, near Dmitri.

When he heard of Tatani's departure, Orschanow felt bitter indignation and rage. He had been painfully, almost unbearably unhappy, but in the face of a *fait accompli*, sanctioned by law, he was impotent. Any initiative on his part would have worsened Tatani's fate. But he resolved to see her again. After each day's hard labour, he would spend the evening prowling around Ben-Ziane's isolated *gourbi*. This quite wealthy man, a stranger to the tribe, had married Tatani because he liked the look of her, without being bothered about other people's opinions, and he guarded her jealously. But sometimes he had to go off to distant markets and spend the night away, and then he would leave Tatani in the care of an old relative who would fall asleep at nightfall, oblivious to everything as long as she wasn't disturbed.

As soon as Tatani learned that Dmitri was watching her at night, she grew bolder, and one night she went out to meet him. In the darkness, they called softly to each other. Dmitri clutched her in his arms, and together they wept over their distress at being parted. Since that night Dmitri had been in unspeakable torment. The only thing that kept him going was his frustrated desire, and his daily hope of seeing Tatani. But their meetings were few and far between, and Dmitri was becoming exhausted by spending all his nights on the lookout, sometimes falling asleep in the wet grass, or in the rain, or in the wind, which was getting colder. But he waited there steadfastly, trembling at the least noise, sometimes calling softly. Nothing interested him any more unless it was to do with Tatani.

He did his work mechanically, almost unconsciously. His *gourbi* was falling apart around him and he didn't bother to repair it. He neglected his appearance, and everyone guessed, from this sudden change alone, the secret of his love affair. Sometimes, after nights of agony, horrible nights when she didn't come, disturbing ideas began to torment him. He felt stirring within him the monster which sleeps in every man. He would have liked to appease it by murder, would have liked to kill this Ben-Ziane, this usurper, and take her back, since she was his! Sometimes Ben-Ziane passed by the farm. He was tall and strong, with an eagle's profile and long, wild eyes with a harsh, cruel and daring look in them.

So, at its first contact with brutal reality, all the glorious artificial edifice which Dmitri called his moral equilibrium had crumbled miserably. He began to see his mistake, to understand that no one, and he no more than anyone else, could free himself from the unknown, tyrannical laws which shape our earthly destinies. But he felt so agitated and confused that he could do nothing about it.

They had one or two more furtive meetings. How much closer their suffering had brought them! How much better, more poignantly, they understood and loved each other since their carefree happiness had been destroyed!

*

The sun was setting as Dmitri came back from the fields. Night was about to fall, and he might see Tatani again. Beyond that, nothing existed. As he was leading the bullocks to their trough, he heard two gunshots. A few minutes later, some men came up the road shouting.

Salah, the native rural policeman, ran into the courtyard

calling for M. Moret. 'Ben-Ziane has killed his wife, Tatani bent Kaddour, with two shots from his gun . . .' He ran off without finishing. Dmitri stood rooted to the spot, stupefied and dazed with horror. Then he felt an acute pain as he realised that he himself was the assassin, that, under the pretext of loving Tatani, but in reality for the satisfaction of his selfish passion, he had condemned her to death!

As if in a dream, Dmitri followed the farm people as they ran over the fields towards the *gourbi*. Outside, sitting on a stone, his wrists chained together, the handsome Ben-Ziane was being guarded by the policeman and two Bedouins. The *caïd* was writing a hurried report. The crowd had reached the *gourbi*, and the women were grieving over the corpse laid out on the ground. Mme Moret had discovered Tatani's body. Pale, her eyes closed, her mouth half-open, the young woman seemed to be sleeping. On her pink *gandoura*, brown stains showed where the two bullets had struck her breast. The relative was telling what had happened. Ben-Ziane had unexpectedly returned from Cavaignac market some hours early, and another tenant-farmer had told him that, the previous evening, he had seen his wife leave the *gourbi* in the night and meet a man in the fields. No doubt the man was Tatani's former lover, the Russian. When he reached home, Ben-Ziane had examined his wife's clothes and shoes: everything had mud marks on it. He pushed her against the wall of the house and shot her point-blank.

Ben-Ziane's eyes remained fixed obstinately in front of him, shining with a dark pride. And Dmitri realised that his duty would be to tell the truth to the assizes so that this man would not be condemned mercilessly. He hadn't the strength to stay any longer, and he left, knowing that from now on he was indifferent to everything, and no longer desired anything. His life had fallen apart, and he was crushed, with nothing left except sorrow and remorse.

*

The road winds over reddish, leprous hills, between black lentisks and tough dwarf palms. Under his blue greatcoat, Dmitri Orschanow walks slowly along the grey road, resigned and at peace now forever, watching the red sun setting and the earth darkening.

After his final attempt at a free life had crumbled, Dmitri had understood that he had no place amongst men, for he could only ever be either their victim or their executioner. He had come back to the Legion with only one desire: to stay forever, and one day to sleep in the corner reserved for the *Heimatlos* in the cemetery in Saïda.

THE HOGARTH PRESS

This is a paperback list for today's readers – but it holds to a tradition of adventurous and original publishing set by Leonard and Virginia Woolf when they founded The Hogarth Press in 1917 and started their first paperback series in 1924.

Some of the books are light-hearted, some serious, and include Fiction, Lives and Letters, Travel, Critics, Poetry, History and Hogarth Crime and Gaslight Crime.

A list of our books already published, together with some of our forthcoming titles, follows. If you would like more information about Hogarth Press books, write to us for a catalogue:

30 Bedford Square, London WC1B 3RP

Please send a large stamped addressed envelope

Robert Louis Stevenson
Island Nights' Entertainments

New Introduction by Lisa St Aubin de Terán

'A literary masterpiece' – Lisa St Aubin de Terán

Heady with the scent and colour of the South Seas and Stevenson's extraordinary talent, here are three of his best tales. A trader tricks a local beauty into a phoney marriage; a Samoan idler finds a fortune in California; a young couple battle with invisible wizards. Anticipating the magical realism of modern fiction, these stories cross the mysterious gulfs between the islanders and the white men who invade their lives, and take us, mesmerised, into the unknown.

Claud Cockburn
Beat the Devil

New Introduction by Alexander Cockburn

In *Beat the Devil* the scene is set for a classic thriller of suspense, romance and hilarity – one which would make the Café Madagascar almost as chic as Rick's in Casablanca. The cast includes: Harry Chelm, the beautiful blond Englishman, every bit as dumb as he seems; Chelm's ravishing young liar of a wife; assorted seedy entrepreneurs; and, of course, the ebullient, epicurean Dannreuthers. All are seeking vast fortunes in the Belgian Congo. All are stranded in the south of France. Tempers fray, passions fester, and suspicions abound in the heat of the midday sun.

Made into a film starring Humphrey Bogart by John Huston, *Beat the Devil* is a timeless cult novel – sophisticated, sardonic, and bursting with intrigue; a splendid entertainment in the best tradition of Graham Greene.

Edwin Muir

The Marionette

New Introduction by Paul Binding

Young Hans Scheffer rambles alone through his father's
house in Salzburg – until he discovers the puppet
theatre . . .

With intense, unnerving clarity, Edwin Muir calls up the
pangs of adolescence, the isolation of madness, the
intoxication of the artist. This simple, shocking story is
unlike anything you have ever read before – or will again.

Ralph Bates
The Olive Field

New Introduction by Valentine Cunningham

First published in 1936, on the eve of the Spanish Civil War, *The Olive Field* tells the immortal tale of two men in love with the same woman. But in the new Spanish Republic personal rivalries soon become entangled with political passions, and the trio find themselves swept into the violence which flares across the land, from the terraced hillsides of Andalusia to northern mines and city streets.

Tender and disturbing, yet as sharply realised as a documentary, *The Olive Field* is a classic novel of the people – one which has been aptly compared to the works of Silone, Malraux and Hemingway.